"You want to... marry me?"

Francesca's eyes slowly opened wide as she stared at him.

"More than anything in the world," Sam said in simple assurance.

Her voice changing, becoming harsh, Francesca said curtly, "You think because I let you kiss me, I want to marry you? You must be crazy! I've had one disastrous marriage and I sure as hell don't intend to make the same mistake again."

Part 2 of Sally Wentworth's
Ties of Passion:

First there was Chris, now we meet his spirited sister Francesca—and see the glamorous world of the Brodeys through her eyes!

Dear Reader,

The wild and primitive scenery of the Douro valley.
The white baroque palaces. What men would live and
rule here? Calum came first, a tall and golden god,
but then Francesca pushed her way into my mind.
Then Chris, very much a man of the world. A family,
then—outwardly tamed, but with hidden emotions as
deep and hot-blooded as the land they lived in. Three
cousins who filled my imagination—fascinating,
absorbing, clamoring to come alive. And three wishes
that had to come true. Then I thought of an
anniversary, and saw a girl, sitting entirely alone
on the riverbank....

Sally Wentworth

Books by Sally Wentworth

HARLEQUIN PRESENTS

1605—THE WAYWARD WIFE
1634—MIRRORS OF THE SEA
1668—YESTERDAY'S AFFAIR
1701—PRACTISE TO DECEIVE
1738—SHADOW PLAY
1764—DUEL IN THE SUN
1787—TO HAVE AND TO HOLD
1810—ONE NIGHT OF LOVE
1832—CHRIS

Look out for the third part of Sally Wentworth's
Ties of Passion series next month: CALUM (#1843).

SALLY WENTWORTH

Francesca

Harlequin Books

TORONTO • NEW YORK • LONDON
AMSTERDAM • PARIS • SYDNEY • HAMBURG
STOCKHOLM • ATHENS • TOKYO • MILAN
MADRID • WARSAW • BUDAPEST • AUCKLAND

RECYCLED PAPER · RECYCLED PAPER

ISBN 0-373-11837-6

FRANCESCA

First North American Publication 1996.

Copyright © 1995 by Sally Wentworth.

This edition published by arrangement with Harlequin Books S.A.

® and TM are trademarks of the publisher. Trademarks indicated with
® are registered in the United States Patent and Trademark Office, the
Canadian Trade Marks Office and in other countries.

Printed in U.S.A.

BRODEY HOUSE BICENTENNIAL

The magnificent eight-eenth-century baroque palace of the Brodey family, situated on the banks of the River Douro in Portugal, will soon be *en fête* for a whole week to celebrate the two hun-dredth anniversary of their company.

The House of Brodey, famous the world over for its fine wines, especially port and Madeira, has now diversified into many other commodities and is one of the biggest family-owned companies in Europe. Originally founded in the beautiful island of Madeira, the company spread to Oporto when Calum Lennox Brodey the first went there two centuries ago to purchase thousands of acres of land in the picturesque Douro valley. That land is now covered with the millions of grape-vines that produce the port on which the family fortune is based.

A FAMILY AFFAIR

Just like any family, every member of the Brodey clan will be in Oporto to welcome their guests from all over the world to the festivities.

Patriarch of the family, Calum Lennox Brodey, named after his ancestor, as are all the eldest sons in the main line, is reported to be greatly looking forward not only to the celebrations but also to the family reunion. Old Calum, as he's popularly known in wine-growing circles, is in his eighties now but still takes a keen interest in the wine-producing side of the company, and is often to be seen by his admiring workers strolling among the vines to check on the crop or tasting the vintage in the family's bottling plant near Oporto.

STILL HAUNTED BY THE PAST

Although the anniversary will be a happy one, in the past there has been terrible tragedy within the family. Some twenty-two years ago Old Calum's two eldest sons and their wives were involved in a fatal car-smash while on holiday in Spain, all four being killed. Each couple had a son of roughly the same age and Old Calum bravely overcame his grief as he took the boys into his palace and brought them up himself, both of them eventually following in his footsteps by joining the company.

It was rumoured at the time of this overwhelmingly tragic accident that old Mr Brodey looked to his third son, Paul,

to help run the business. Paul Brodey, however, was hooked on painting and is now a celebrated artist. He lives near Lisbon with his wife Maria, who is half Portuguese and is herself a well-known painter. The good news is, though, that their only child, Christopher, has joined the family firm on the sales side and is based mainly in New York.

Only one of Old Calum's grandsons now shares the splendour of the palace, which is mainly decorated in Renaissance style, with him. This is the only child of his late eldest son, who, following the family tradition, is also called Calum—Young Calum, in this case. The younger Calum Brodey, around thirty years old and one of the most eligible bachelors in the country, if not in Europe, has virtually taken over the running of the company, but will be gracefully taking a back seat to his grandfather during the week's festivities.

SALLY WENTWORTH 7

MARRIAGE IN MIND?

Another extraordinary tradition peculiar to the family is that all the men maintain their links with their mother country by marrying blonde English girls. Every son of the family for the past several generations has travelled to the UK and returned with a beautiful 'English rose' on his arm. Will Young Calum and Christopher carry on the tradition, we wonder?

The third Brodey grandson, Lennox, who now lives in Madeira with his beautiful and adored wife Stella, who is expecting their first child later this year, will be among the family guests. Stella, of course, is a blonde and lovely English girl.

Old Calum's fourth child, his elegant daughter Adele, is married to the well-known French millionaire, the gallant and still handsome Guy de Charenton, an assiduous worker for the Paris Opera and for the many charities that he supports.

Although the Brodey family has many connections with the upper echelons of society, especially in England, it was Adele's daughter and only child, the sensationally beautiful Francesca, who finally linked it to the aristocracy with her marriage to Prince Paolo de Vieira a few years ago. This marriage, which took place in the Prince's fairy-tale castle in Italy, looked all set to have the proverbial happy ending, but, alas, this wasn't to be and the couple parted after only two years. Since then Francesca's name has been linked with several men, including lately Michel, the Comte de la Fontaine, seen with her on her many shopping trips in Paris and Rome.

To all the glamorous members of the Brodey family we extend our warm congratulations on their anniversary, and we are sure that all their lucky guests will have the most lavish and memorable time at the bicentennial celebrations.

THE HOUSE OF BRODEY

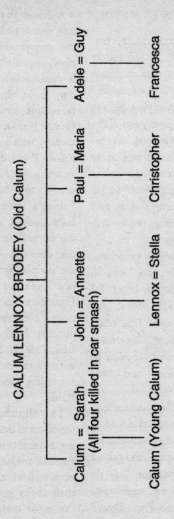

CALUM LENNOX BRODEY (Old Calum)

Calum = Sarah
(All four killed in car smash)

John = Annette

Paul = Maria

Adele = Guy

Calum (Young Calum)

Lennox = Stella

Christopher

Francesca

CHAPTER ONE

THEY were all there—the Brodeys—gathered together in the beautiful gardens of their magnificent baroque *palácio* near Oporto. All of them had come to celebrate the two hundredth anniversary of the House of Brodey.

Even Francesca, the princess, was there.

Calum Lennox Brodey, the head of his house and an old man now, looked across at his only granddaughter with a mixture of pride and exasperation. Tall and fair, slim and elegant, she was as beautiful as any man could wish his descendant to be. She was also totally spoilt, by him as much as by her parents, he had to admit that, and also by the family's wealth and position. A waiter came up and offered him another glass of iced white port, the port grown and matured in the family's own vineyards, here in Portugal, and on which their fortune was based. He took the glass and automatically smelt the richness of the wine before he sipped it.

Several of Old Calum's guests stood around him as he stood and chatted affably, but his eyes often went to where Francesca—in her brightly coloured outfit, followed always by that lap-dog of a French count—also circulated among their guests. The man was all wrong for her, of course, just as her ex-husband had been. But the girl had insisted on marrying her Italian prince. She had a will of her own, and whatever she wanted she always got, including whichever man she wanted. Except once. Not that getting her own way seemed to have made her happy, he thought with an inner sigh.

9

Unaware of her grandfather's thoughts, Francesca was enjoying herself. It was good to be back at the *palácio* where she had spent so many happy holidays in the past; good to be with her Brodey relations for this week of festivities, a lunch party for people in the wine trade, many of whom would be staying in Oporto for the whole week so that they could also attend the gala ball which was to be the highlight of the celebrations.

Glancing round to see that everything was going well, Francesca caught her grandfather's eye and smiled at him. She was tall enough to do so, taller than many of the guests, and able to see over their heads. Noticing some people standing apart at the far end of the lawn, she excused herself from the group she was with and began to walk towards them, taking a glass of port from a waiter as she did so. Michel followed her and put a hand on her shoulder to stop her.

'Francesca, *chérie*, why don't you show me round these beautiful gardens? No one will miss us for a few minutes. There is something that I wish to ask you.' He gave her one of his most charming smiles. 'Something, I think, that your family would——'

But she shook him off before he could finish. She wasn't in the mood and was already wishing that she hadn't invited him to the party. Not only this party: he too was staying for the whole week. She could have refused to invite him, she supposed, but she had been seeing so much of him lately and he'd said that it would be a good opportunity for him to meet her family. And to sum up how much they were worth, she thought cynically.

Coming up to the guests who were standing apart, she gave them a warm smile and said, 'Hello, I'm Francesca de Vieira, Calum Brodey's granddaughter. I don't think we've met.'

She was good at putting people at their ease, good at being sociable. Her mother had beautiful manners and had instilled them into her from childhood. Her parents were here somewhere, working their way through the guests, as they all were. Her mother, though, was still angry with her at the moment, hadn't yet forgiven her for divorcing the prince and the unwelcome publicity surrounding it. But she was more angry at the divorce than the publicity, Francesca thought fairly. Her mother didn't believe in divorce. Nor did Francesca, if it came to that; but when living with someone got to the stage when you dreaded the hell of each new day, then the only way out was a divorce. She would have done it cleanly, but Paolo, angry and vindictive, had made it messy.

The gossip papers were now saying that she would marry Michel—the Comte de la Fontaine, to give him his full title. She wasn't yet sure herself whether she was going to or not. He was a little old for her—in his late thirties compared to her twenty-four—but he was good-looking and charming in a very French way, and kept himself very fit. And he was, of course, tall—an important factor when she was so tall herself. But maybe she shouldn't have let him persuade her into inviting him this week. In Paris, Michel had been entertaining enough; here, alongside her cousins, he somehow seemed completely out of place. Perhaps it would have been better to have a break from him, so that she could think about what she wanted to do.

Before long, other guests had drifted to join the group round her. Mostly men, attracted by her beauty, by her title, her status, and also by one or two revelations the prince had made about their private life and which the gossip columns had snapped up. But then, Francesca had always attracted men; unfortunately she was beginning to find that they no longer attracted her. Maybe that was what a bad marriage did for you. Maybe Michel really was in love with her, as he kept saying he was, and wasn't thinking about his château back in France that was badly in need of repair.

There were other men, too, who had tried to get close to her since her marriage had ended, some even before it had ended. All of them moved in the jet-set circles of various countries of which she had become a part, but sometimes it seemed as if every man was the same and there was none that she could really trust, none that she was sure wanted her only for herself.

Only when she was with her big Brodey cousins could she really relax. The four of them—herself, Young Calum, Chris and Lennox—had spent part of every year together here when they were children, under their grandfather's genial, easygoing wing. They had run through the gardens, sailed on the river, worked on the grape-vines in the *quintas*, treading the grapes when the harvest was done. She was the youngest, and of course the only girl, so her cousins had looked after her, treating her rather like an appealing puppy who followed them and wouldn't be left behind.

Thinking of her cousins, Francesca looked round for them. Calum was over on the far side of the garden, surrounded by people, and Lennox was fetching a chair for his wife, Stella, who was pregnant with their first child. Marriage had transformed Lennox; prior to meeting Stella, he had been becoming withdrawn, away on his island of Madeira, but he was now so much in love, so overwhelmingly happy, that he wanted the whole

world to share it. Francesca smiled as she watched him,
then turned to look for Chris, the last of her cousins.
He was threading his way through the crowd towards
her, and she gave him a warm smile of greeting, then
noticed that he had a girl with him. The girl was blonde,
petite, and very attractive. Attractive to Chris at any rate;
Francesca could read it in his eyes.

'Francesca, this is Tiffany Dean. My cousin, the
Princess de Vieira,' he said formally.

'You're so lucky to be tall, Princess,' the girl said to
her as they shook hands.

'Please, call me Francesca. And I don't consider it an
advantage. Think what a choice of men you have compared to me.'

They laughed and looked each other over with the
brief, indirect glances women used when they were
summing each other up, taking in looks, clothes, manner,
and coming to an instantaneous opinion on status that
was so often right. Compared to Francesca's flame-
coloured trouser-suit, Tiffany was very conservatively
dressed in a grey silk suit, and had a shining bell of
smooth blonde hair. She looked like a lovely and fragile
doll, and made Francesca feel about ten feet tall. She
thought that Chris had brought Tiffany to the party, but
it seemed that she was here by invitation.

Francesca started to talk to Chris, teasing him, making
him grin, but Michel got tired of being ignored and drew
her attention to the rest of the guests, who were making
their way to another part of the garden where tables had
been set for lunch.

'The buffet is about to be served. Where do you wish
to sit?' he said in French.

Annoyed at his interruption, annoyed that she'd been
fool enough to let him come, Francesca snapped back

in the same language, 'If you're hungry, then go and eat. I'll come when I'm ready.'

He didn't go away, of course, just stood there with ostentatious patience while Tiffany put herself out to be entertaining. She did it well, Francesca had to admit as she laughed and listened. She began to like Tiffany, and could see that Chris did too; he hardly took his eyes off the girl. A spark of hidden desolation ran through Francesca; it was bad enough having Lennox married; if Chris and Calum got married as well, she would lose them all, lose the special relationship that had built up between them over the years. No matter that theirs was only a platonic relationship, that it was only cousinly love they felt; it went back as far as she could remember and in some ways was stronger and deeper than any marriage bond could be.

The garden was almost empty now; it was time to break this up. Michel was still standing beside her, so there was no getting rid of him. 'I suppose we'd better go and eat,' she said to him. But she wanted to sit with Chris and Calum, so she invited Tiffany to join them, knowing that Chris would come too. 'Tiffany, you will come and sit with us, won't you? Now, where's Calum?' she asked, looking round.

She saw him across the garden and began to move in his direction. Calum noticed and came across, grinned back at her when she smiled at him, but shook his head when she raised an eyebrow in invitation. 'Remember Grandfather wants us to split up,' he reminded her.

Francesca put her arm through his, demonstrating her right to get close to her handsome cousin, and said coaxingly, 'Do we have to? I haven't seen you or Chris for simply ages. I'd much rather sit with you both.'

Calum covered her hand with his and gave her one of the special smiles that he kept for her—and small animals that he found amusing and lovable. 'We can catch up on all our news over dinner tonight.'

'But Grandfather will be there, and you can't *really* talk when he's listening. The dear old darling gets so upset if you tell the truth, the whole truth and nothing but the truth. Not to mention the parents,' she added feelingly.

Calum smiled but said in mock-admonition, 'You shouldn't lead such a wild life.'

Realising that she wasn't going to get her own way, Francesca dropped his arm and said, 'All right, we'll split up. I'm so sorry, Tiffany,' she said, turning to Tiffany. 'Now you'll have to put up with Chris. How boring for you.'

Chris gave her an injured look. 'Hey!' he protested.

Calum laughed, and asked to be introduced to Tiffany. Chris was about to do so when another man, a stranger, walked up to them.

'Tiffany! So there you are. I'm afraid the ice in your drink melted so I drank it myself,' the man said with a drawling American accent.

For a moment Tiffany was unable to hide the consternation in her eyes. Francesca noticed and her female intuition was immediately aroused. Why had the other girl reacted like that? Something was wrong here. Looking at the man with some curiosity, she saw that he was as tall as her cousin Calum, but where Calum's hair was fair this man's was dark and thick. His eyes, long-lashed and lazy-lidded, were also dark, and his shoulders were very broad, as if he was used to doing tough, manual work.

From the surprise in his eyes and the way he stiffened, it was obvious that Chris knew nothing about him. The smile faded in Calum's face, too, as he realised that Tiffany wasn't alone.

'Hi there,' the man added, looking round at them.

A flash of anger shone in Tiffany's eyes, but was quickly covered as she said, 'This is Mr—er—I'm sorry, I can't remember your name. One of your other guests,' she said to Calum.

'It's Gallagher. Sam Gallagher.' The American shook hands with the men, then turned to Francesca. 'I guess you must be the Princess.'

Things were becoming clearer to Francesca now; she guessed that Tiffany had met Sam Gallagher here and had been trying to ditch him. So that she could meet Chris or Calum? Francesca wondered. She began to be amused and intrigued. 'I guess I must be, at that,' she answered. And, wanting to know more, added, 'Have you been looking for Tiffany?'

Sam gave a lazy smile. 'Yeah. I went to get her a drink but she kind of disappeared. Found someone else to talk to, I guess.'

Francesca looked at Chris and raised an enquiring eyebrow. He gave a rueful smile. 'Sorry, I didn't mean to tread on anyone's toes,' he said wryly.

Tiffany smiled at him and made some bright comment, but Chris moved away with Calum, as Francesca had known he would; he wasn't the type to muscle in on another man's territory, especially when that man was a guest at their party.

For a brief moment bitterness showed in Tiffany's eyes. If Francesca hadn't been watching her she might have missed it, because the next second the bright smile was back on the other girl's face and she looked as if she hadn't a care in the world. Her curiosity growing, Francesca decided it might be amusing to follow this through, so said, 'But *we* don't have to split up. Come and sit with Michel and me, Tiffany.' And added, to see how the other girl would react, 'And you too, of course, Mr Gallagher.'

'Sure thing.'

The American put a hand on Tiffany's arm as they made their way across the garden, but she shook him off and gave him a look of dislike that spoke volumes. Sam didn't seem to notice, merely walking along in that loose-limbed way that so many American men seemed to have, his legs so long that Tiffany couldn't keep up.

There were people sitting at most of the tables but Francesca deliberately walked to one where there were pairs of vacant seats almost opposite each other across the round table. That way she could watch Sam and Tiffany, see how they reacted to one another. Although it had been swiftly hidden, Tiffany was obviously angry with Sam for taking her away from Chris, although it seemed that both men had been strangers to her before today.

Francesca glanced at Sam, thinking how different from Michel he was—the Frenchman with his lean Gallic features, his suave charm born of centuries of noble blood, the American with the look of craggy toughness about him, the air of being quietly able to handle any situation. The latter was younger than Michel—about thirty, Francesca guessed, and definitely not one of the international jet set. She wasn't quite sure how she knew; perhaps it was just something about him, as if he found this kind of party pleasant enough but was there more as an onlooker than a participant.

Calum and the last of the guests had come to take their seats, but to Francesca's consternation she saw that they were one place-setting short at the last table to be filled. Quickly she got to her feet to attend to it, but Calum had already beckoned a waiter over and he was laying an extra place. The head of the catering company, Elaine Beresford, had also seen and came up to Francesca.

'I laid exactly the number of places you wanted, Francesca,' she said with a frown. 'A hundred and sixty. It worked out so well: sixteen tables each of ten people.'

'Perhaps there's an empty place at one of the other tables?' Francesca suggested.

'No, I've checked; they're all full. There's definitely one more guest here than on your seating list.'

'How strange. Perhaps someone refused and then changed their mind and turned up. Well, it can't be helped.' Francesca went back to her seat, thinking that at a party like this, where there were so many people she didn't know, it would be impossible to find out who the extra person was. Strangers like Tiffany and Sam, she thought, glancing at them and for the first time wondering just how they both came to be invited to a party for people in the wine trade.

Watching them covertly as the meal progressed, Francesca saw that Tiffany gave Sam the cold shoulder for a while but then relented and began to chat with him. Sam was talking, his deep voice carrying across the table. He was telling Tiffany about cattle-ranching in the States, about stampedes and rodeos, speaking eloquently, holding the other girl's interest and making her laugh. Perhaps now she was pleased that Sam had taken her away from Chris. Tiffany glanced across at her and Francesca looked at Sam and raised an eyebrow a fraction—a very slight movement but one that Tiffany had no trouble at all in interpreting. She shook her head, denying an interest in Sam, denying any attraction for him despite his good looks and easy manner.

The meal over, the guests got to their feet and began to mingle again as the waiters served glasses of vintage port to round off the meal. Abandoning Michel, Francesca went to look for Chris. She found him at the other side of the garden, talking to some Australian buyers. Francesca gave them one of her most dazzling smiles. 'You will forgive me if I steal my cousin from you for a moment, won't you? There's something terribly important that I have to ask him.'

They couldn't refuse, of course, so Francesca put her arm through Chris's and drew him away.

'And what is this terribly important question?'

'Oh, there isn't one. I just thought I'd rescue you from a boring conversation.'

'It wasn't boring. And anyway, how do you know I won't be bored talking to you?' he teased.

She wrinkled her nose at him. 'Even when Paolo got really mad at me, he had to admit that I was never boring,' she told him, referring to her ex-husband.

Chris gave her a contemplative look. She very seldom spoke of Paolo or of her marriage; maybe the fact that she'd done so now meant that she was starting to get over it at last. 'Do you ever see him?' he asked her, feeling his way.

'Good heavens, no!' She gave a brittle laugh. 'And I never want to. I should never have married him.'

'Why did you, then?'

But she didn't want to talk about it, so said, 'It was on the rebound, of course—from you and Calum and Lennox.'

'From us!' Chris exclaimed.

'Yes, I was so afraid of ending up with someone as arrogant and chauvinistic as you three that I went to the other extreme.'

Chris bunched his fist and pretended to punch her on the jaw. 'Just watch it. Princess or no, I can still put you over my knee and give you a spanking.'

She laughed up at him. 'So that's what turns you on, huh?'

But Chris had glanced away and she saw him frown. Tiffany had come from the house into the garden and Sam, who had just been given a glass of port by Calum, walked over to her. He leaned close to her, said something.

The sound of the slap that Tiffany gave him echoed round the garden and was so alien that everyone stopped talking and turned to look. 'How dare you?' she cried out.

Chris stiffened in amazement, then shook off Francesca's arm to hurry towards them, as did Calum from the opposite direction. Tiffany turned from Sam and ran, not towards Chris, but to Calum, which Francesca found an interesting move.

Calum put himself between her and Sam and with all the coldness of an affronted host said, 'My cousin will escort you to the gate.'

Sam started to protest but Chris took his arm to lead him away. For a moment it seemed as if Sam was going to resist, but then he gave Tiffany a long look before shrugging in an angry way and letting Chris escort him out of the garden. Francesca watched them go thoughtfully, wondering what Sam had said to merit a slap in such a public place. From what she'd seen of him he didn't look the kind to do anything so uncivilised, so foolish. Maybe the wine had got to him; there had certainly been plenty of it served at lunch. But then Francesca remembered the look that had been in Tiffany's eyes when he'd started to protest. It had been almost a look of appeal, certainly not one of insult and outrage.

More intrigued than ever, Francesca decided that she would help this game along to see what would happen, so she went to Tiffany and said, 'Perhaps you'd better come inside with me,' and, when Tiffany said she'd wait until Sam had gone, she pointed at the stain on her suit where Sam's port had spilt down the skirt.

'Oh, no!' There was genuine distress in her voice as Tiffany saw it.

'Come into the house. I'm sure we can save it if we do something quickly.'

Calum added his urging voice to Francesca's and the two girls went into the house together and up to one of the guest bedrooms. Francesca found a bathrobe for Tiffany and sent for a maid who took the skirt away to be cleaned.

'I do hope it comes out,' Tiffany said anxiously.

Her anxiety was interesting; either she was extremely caring about her clothes or else she didn't have many decent things to care about. Francesca would have liked to find out which, but had to hurry back down to the party to stand at Calum's side and say goodbye to the other guests until the garden was at last clear.

Chris walked back from the entrance and came over to them.

'Did you see Gallagher off the premises?' Calum asked him. And when Chris nodded he said angrily, 'How the hell did he get in here? I've never seen him before and

I'm sure he can't have had an invitation. He must have been the extra guest—or gatecrasher, more like.'

'What extra guest?'

Calum explained and Chris looked thoughtful but shook his head. 'No, he had an invitation. I asked him and he showed it to me. But it was made out for someone else—an American shipper. Gallagher said the other man couldn't come so passed the invitation on to him.'

'I hope you told him that he wouldn't be welcome here again,' Calum said tersely. 'I won't have our guests insulted like that.'

'Did he say anything?' Francesca asked Chris. 'Say that it was a misunderstanding, or anything?'

'He wasn't very pleased at being made to leave, that was evident, but he was tight-lipped about it. I tried to get him to give an explanation but he wouldn't.'

'How strange,' Francesca commented. 'Most men in that situation would be protesting their innocence all the way down the drive.'

'Hardly, when it was so obvious that whatever he said was far from innocent,' Calum said wryly. He turned to Francesca. 'Is Tiffany all right?'

'Just upset about her suit. I've left her in one of the guest rooms while it's being cleaned.'

'Ask her to come down, will you? I'll be in the sitting-room.'

'I'll come with you,' Chris said, and the two cousins walked into the house.

Francesca went back upstairs, thinking about Sam Gallagher. If he'd had a genuine invitation, that still left Tiffany; could she be the gatecrasher? Maybe if she was asked a few judicious questions it would be possible to find out; it would be interesting, too, to learn exactly what Sam had said to deserve that slap across the face.

She found Tiffany seated on the edge of the four-poster bed, wrapped in the bathrobe, which was much too big for her, looking rather lost and forlorn. Her air of vulnerability threw Francesca for a moment; she looked too innocent to be anything but what she appeared to be. But it was only for a moment. Francesca made some small talk about her grandfather, then sat on the bed next to Tiffany, determined to find out what she could.

'You must be feeling wretched...' she said consolingly. 'The stupid man! Why don't they ever learn? You only have to smile at them and be friendly and they immediately think you're willing to leap into bed with them. And Sam seemed OK, too. Just shows you how mistaken you can be.'

A flush of colour crept into the other girl's cheeks. Could it be guilt? And she quickly changed the subject, making Francesca wonder if the slap had been a ploy, especially when Tiffany asked if she could stay until her suit was dry.

'Of course. But you can't possibly spend the whole afternoon in here. I'd lend you something of mine but you'd be swamped in it.' An idea came to her and Francesca added, 'But I'll see what I can arrange.' She stood up. 'Calum wants to speak to you. He's downstairs.'

Tiffany's face lightened and she sat up straighter. 'What about?'

'He didn't tell me. He never does. Come and see,' Francesca said with a shrug.

'Like this? I can't possibly,' Tiffany protested, but she got to her feet.

'Of course you can. Calum won't care.'

Francesca doubted if she herself would have gone down to see a comparative stranger, in a strange house,

dressed like that, but Tiffany followed her without any
further protest. She didn't even bother to put on her
shoes, so that the robe trailed almost to the ground as
they went down to the sitting-room where the men were
waiting.

Both of them smiled when they saw Tiffany in the
over-sized robe, and she seemed to come alive, making
a joke of it and twirling round to draw even more attention to it.

Calum came forward to apologise to her, took her
hand. 'Miss Dean, I'd like to apologise to you on behalf
of my family. We're all extremely sorry that such a thing
happened here.'

Tiffany flushed attractively, disclaimed, and Francesca
began to think that she was either very innocent or very
clever. Calum seemed taken—and taken in—by her, but
when Francesca glanced at Chris she saw that there was
a sardonic look in his eyes as he watched them, so maybe
he too was beginning to think it was a charade.

But then Tiffany said to Calum, 'Oh, please, don't
apologise. I probably over-reacted. After all, I had been
sitting next to Mr Gallagher during lunch, and—well, in
a way I suppose it's your fault really—you *do* serve ex-
cellent wine!'

This made them all laugh, including Francesca, despite her suspicions, and even had Chris raise his eyebrows in surprise.

'And such a lot of it,' Francesca said, her mind suddenly full of doubts as she began to think that maybe
she'd been wrong in her suspicions.

'You're being extremely good about it,' Calum said,
smiling warmly. 'But you must let us make it up to you.
Perhaps we could——'

But Francesca, not knowing whether to feel guilty or wary, and wanting to find out one way or the other, said quickly, 'I know; you must join us for dinner tonight!'

Calum was taken aback but had to go along with it and added his voice to the invitation. Tiffany protested, but in such a half-hearted way that it was obvious she liked the idea; not that it proved anything, of course. Francesca waited for Tiffany to accept, to ask someone to take her home so that she could change, but Tiffany said laughingly, 'But how can I possibly?' and indicated the bathrobe.

'Oh, that's easily solved. I'll ring a boutique in the town and tell them to bring up a selection of gowns for you to choose from. They should be here before too long,' Francesca said after a moment's hesitation, watching for Tiffany's reaction.

It was a far from ordinary offer, and one which few women that Francesca knew would have accepted, but a look almost of relief came into Tiffany's face. She made another very half-hearted protest to Calum, and took the opportunity to flirt with him a little before finally being persuaded to stay. But now Francesca was quite sure that she had been eager to accept all along.

Calum went out to tell the staff to lay another place for dinner, and Francesca went over to the phone to call the boutique. But Chris moved, attracting her attention, and by the smallest movement of his eyebrow indicated that he wanted her to leave him alone with Tiffany.

'The number is in my address book upstairs,' Francesca improvised. 'Will you excuse me while I go and make the call?' and she went out of the room, leaving them together.

Francesca would dearly have loved to listen at the keyhole. Maybe she would be able to get Chris to tell

her afterwards, although she very much doubted it; all
three of her cousins tended to treat her like an indulged
younger sister, but now that they were mature men she
could no longer charm their secrets out of them as she'd
used to. What they didn't want her to know, they kept
to themselves. She rang the best boutique in Oporto,
telling them to bring a selection of day and evening
clothes for Tiffany as soon as possible.

Her bedroom, with the four-poster bed draped in
delicate, flower-printed fabric, was the one she'd always
occupied since she'd first come here as a child. It looked
out over the garden at the rear of the house and was
almost over the sitting-room where Chris was talking to
Tiffany. It evidently hadn't been a long conversation because she soon saw Chris come out on to the terrace.
Peeping out of her door, Francesca saw Tiffany come
up the stairs and go to the spare room again. As soon
as the other girl had closed the door behind her,
Francesca ran downstairs and out into the garden.

'Chris!'

He turned and waited as she ran towards him.

'Well?' she demanded impatiently when he didn't
speak. 'What happened between you and Tiffany?'

'Happened?' He shrugged. 'Nothing.'

'Chris, that isn't fair. Why did you signal me to leave
you alone with her, then?'

He gave her an amused look out of cool grey eyes.
'Maybe I just wanted the opportunity to get to know
her better.'

'So why cut it short? You were only together for a
few minutes.'

'Sometimes a few minutes is all it takes.'

Exasperated, Francesca caught his arm and shook it.
'Stop being so damn enigmatic. Do you fancy her?'

'Of course—but then I fancy most women. Except you, naturally.'

'Don't try to change the subject. Come on, Chris, you can tell me,' she said coaxingly.

He laughed. 'Oh, no, that tone doesn't work on me; I know you too well.'

Francesca tried another tactic. Pulling him down to sit beside her on one of the stone seats overlooking the gardens, she said, 'Lennox looks so happy, don't you think? Marriage really suits him. Maybe we ought to try and marry Calum off as well.' Testing the ground, she went on, 'How about Tiffany? She's a blonde. And all you male Brodeys are supposed to marry blondes, remember.'

She was watching him closely and saw his eyebrows flicker at the coupling of Calum and Tiffany's names, but then Chris gave a short laugh. 'That old wives' tale! You don't really expect any of us to take any notice of it, do you?'

'Lennox married a blonde.'

'Purely a coincidence. Anyone can see he's head over heels in love with Stella. He'd have married her whatever the colour of her hair.'

Bringing him back to the point, Francesca said, 'Well, you might not care about the family tradition—after all, your father didn't—but Calum will follow it, I think. And Tiffany's coming along might be fate. I think he quite likes her,' she said pensively. 'Don't you?'

Chris shrugged and moved rather restlessly. 'He only met her this afternoon, for God's sake.'

'Ah, yes, but you just said that sometimes a few minutes is all it takes,' she reminded him with a mischievous smile.

He had to grin back. 'Hoist with my own cliché,' he said with a mock-groan.

'Seriously, though, don't you think that Calum and Tiffany would make a charming couple? I wonder if she fancies him?'

'Well, I expect we'll find out, now that you've more or less insisted she stay to dinner.'

'It was the least we could do after what happened at the party,' Francesca said innocently.

'Rubbish! You've decided to meddle, play a game of your own.'

'What game could I possibly play?' she protested.

'Matchmaking?' Chris gave her an assessing look. 'But no. I don't somehow think that you'd be an advocate of marriage at the moment. So what game are you playing, little cousin?'

'How lovely to be called "little". You three are the only ones who ever do it.'

'How abut your father?' he asked, momentarily diverted.

'Oh, I hardly ever see him. All his time is taken up with directorships of opera houses and art galleries. And Maman is just as bad; she's on so many charity committees that I've lost count. Even when I'm in Paris I hardly ever see them.'

'Ah, poor thing,' Chris said in mock-sympathy.

She laughed obligingly, but it was true; when her marriage had broken up and she'd needed loving sympathy, her parents had given her none. Admittedly, her father had shown no feelings either way, but her mother had been very angry at the break-up and had even urged her to go back to Paolo. Chris had been away in Australia and Lennox in Madeira, so it had been here to her grandfather that Francesca had run. To him and Young

Calum. And it had been these two who had given her
bruised spirit the comfort she needed. She was infinitely
grateful and loved them both very dearly. It was why
she felt so strongly that she would never want to see
either of them hurt.

So maybe it would be best if her suspicions about
Tiffany were brought out into the open now, before any
harm could be done. Turning to Chris, she said directly,
'Do you think that Tiffany gatecrashed our party?'

'Do you?'

She felt a flash of anger at the way he'd sidestepped
the question, but said, 'Yes, I do. And I think we ought
to face her with it.'

She began to get to her feet, but Chris pulled her back.
'No, you don't,' he said firmly.

'But if she——'

'She could be perfectly innocent.'

'Do you really think so?'

He shrugged.

'We know nothing about her. Did she tell you anything?' Francesca persisted.

'She said she works in Oporto. In the commercial
district.'

'For what company?'

'She didn't say.'

'There was no invitation made out in her name. That
I'm sure of.'

'No. She said a colleague in her company passed one
on to her.'

'That's possible, I suppose. But I think we ought to
ask her right out.'

But Chris said firmly, 'No. Give it some more time.
Wait and see what happens.'

'But what if she makes a play for Calum?'

'So let her.'

'But—but I thought you fancied her yourself.'

Chris gave her a glittery kind of smile. 'Maybe Tiffany is the gatecrasher. Maybe she's playing some game of her own. Don't you think it would be rather amusing to find out what it is? Just to go along with it and not ask any awkward questions—before we do anything?'

Francesca stared at him, not having thought her cousin to be that devious before. For a moment she felt reluctance, but she too was full of fascinated curiosity, so she nodded. 'All right. We'll watch—and wait.'

CHAPTER TWO

A MAID came to tell Francesca that the assistant from the boutique had arrived. Francesca gave it half an hour, then went into the spare room that Tiffany was using, wondering if the other girl would offer to pay for the clothes.

Tiffany had chosen a black velvet dress for the evening and was wearing a fashionable shorts-suit which she looked really good in. Francesca admired it and told the assistant to charge the clothes to her account.

'Oh, but really...' Tiffany made a protest that was so half-hearted, she needn't have bothered.

Her theory that Tiffany was just a money-grabber borne out, Francesca said rather tightly, 'No, please. My pleasure. Let's go down, shall we?'

Going down the wide staircase, she tried to find out more about the other girl without making it too obvious that she was probing, first saying where she lived herself, then asking, 'Do you live in Oporto?'

'Yes, I'm sharing a place with friends,' Tiffany replied, but added nothing more.

Remembering Chris's instructions not to ask direct questions, Francesca reluctantly had to leave it at that. They walked to the sitting-room and out on to the terrace where Calum was talking to the caterer.

Coming over to them, Calum said, 'Francesca, do you have any further instructions for Mrs Beresford on the party at the *quinta*?'

31

Francesca did, but was reluctant to leave Calum and Tiffany alone together, despite Chris having told her to let Tiffany have her head. But she stood up and said, 'Yes. Would you excuse me for a moment, Tiffany?'

The girl couldn't wait to get rid of her and be alone with Calum. She had gestured to him to sit next to her even before the other two women had gone back into the house.

Francesca went over to the big desk where she kept the folders containing her copies of the details of the week's festivities, and took out the one for the party for all the estate workers which was to be held at the *quinta* in a couple of days. She began to go through it with Elaine Beresford, but stood so that she could still see Tiffany and Calum. Unfortunately, she couldn't hear what they were saying, but Tiffany was obviously putting herself out to be sparkling and vivacious, and Calum seemed to be agreeably amused by the way he was smiling and laughing. Francesca gritted her teeth, not liking to see her cousin being used in this way. For she was sure now, from the way Tiffany was behaving, that it was Calum she was out to get. She was aiming high—at the heir to most of the Brodey empire, who would one day be one of the richest men in Portugal.

How dared she? Francesca thought, in a sudden burst of disappointment and anger. Was everyone the same— just out for what they could get? First Michel and now Tiffany? The girl had seemed nice at first, but she had more than likely tricked her way into the house and here she was so obviously setting out to entrap Calum. And she was succeeding too, by the look of it. Calum hadn't appeared to be so absorbed in a girl for ages. Francesca's anger deepened; she had a good mind to go out there and tell him, to break it up for good and all!

'Do you know how many fado dancers and singers we'll have to cater for?' Elaine Beresford asked, interrupting her thoughts.

With difficulty, Francesca dragged her mind back and looked again at the folder. 'About twenty, I should think. Then there are all the coach and minibus drivers who are bringing the workers and their families from the other *quintas* in the valley, of course. Oh, and the bullfighters and their assistants.'

'Bullfighters?' Elaine's eyes widened in horror.

'Oh, don't worry, we don't kill the bulls in Portugal,' Francesca assured her. 'In fact, it's forbidden.'

'But the poor horses?' Elaine said.

'We don't use those either. The matadors will be on foot. It's rather like a ballet. All very graceful and very harmless. Really. You must watch it.'

Elaine didn't look very keen on the idea, but turned back to her lists.

Francesca glanced again out at the terrace, realising that the longer the two of them were left together, the more difficult it would be to convince Calum that Tiffany was only out for what she could get. The girl was so plausible. Seemed so genuine. Luckily, Chris strolled into the room so she was able to give him an expressive signal with her eyes. He frowned a little, but then went out on the terrace to join the others. Tiffany looked up, saw him, and was hardly able to hide her annoyance at being interrupted.

With an inner sigh of relief, Francesca gave her attention to the caterer again. But she found that it was Elaine's turn to be abstracted as she too looked out at the terrace where the others were sitting, a pensive look in her eyes.

'Elaine?'

'Oh, sorry.' Elaine blinked, gave Francesca a smile of apology and her full attention.

When all the *quinta* party details had been settled, Francesca went out on to the terrace again and sat down between Calum and Chris. Deliberately she began to talk about mutual friends and relations, people that Tiffany didn't know.

Tiffany sat silently for a while, then stood up, 'What time is dinner?'

'Oh, dear, don't let us drive you away, Tiffany. I'm sorry; it's just that we haven't seen each other for so long. We didn't mean to bore you,' Francesca said, not meaning it. Then she added maliciously, 'Chris, why don't you take Tiffany for a walk round the garden while I catch up on Calum's news? I'll get round to you later.'

Tiffany's face tightened and she started to protest. 'Oh, no, please. I'd just as soon——'

'But I insist,' Chris broke in. 'Francesca can tell me all her secrets later.' And he gave his cousin a sardonic smile.

'What makes you think I have any secrets?' she returned tauntingly.

Chris bent to kiss her cheek. 'Vixen,' he whispered in her ear, then added aloud, 'You always have—and until some man comes along who can tame you you always will.'

'Hark at the man! A psychologist now,' Francesca retorted, wondering if it was true. She added in bravado, 'I'll have you know I've decided to marry Michel.'

'Congratulations. I'll give it six months.'

'Six months!'

'No, perhaps you're right. *Three* months should have you bored to tears and walking out on him.'

Francesca threw a cushion at him but her face tightened; she knew that she was already bored with Michel and wondered if life would ever seem really worth living again. Whether there was any man in the world who could dispel the loneliness in her heart.

When they were out of sight, Calum said, 'Where is Michel, by the way?'

'He went back to his hotel.'

'He could have stayed here, you know; we would have found room for him.'

Shaking her head, Francesca said moodily, 'I didn't want him at the house. I wish now that I'd never let him come here at all.'

'Does that mean that you're not going to marry him?' Calum asked equably.

'No, of course I'm not. I don't know why I even went out with him in the first place. I suppose it was on the rebound from Paolo.' She got restlessly to her feet and strode to the edge of the terrace, and stood there for a moment, then swung round and said almost angrily, 'Why can't I meet someone I can—can respect? Someone like you and Chris and Lennox?'

'We're hardly role models.'

'But you are! You're all three *men*, in every definition of the word. You're in control of your own lives, could have made your own way even without the family business. Why, between the three of you you've spread and doubled the size of the company since Grandfather put it into your hands. You're all so self-assured, so capable. Why can't I meet someone like that?'

Calum got up and came to pull her down to sit beside him on the terrace wall. He put his arm round her as he said comfortingly, 'There's someone out there for you, little one.'

'No, I don't think so.' She raised a strained face to him. 'I've got to fill my life somehow, but I don't know how. Look at Elaine; when her husband was killed she went into business for herself. But I haven't the faintest idea how to do something like that. Sometimes I feel just like a—a picture on the wall: expensive to buy, nice to have and to look at in passing, but no use whatsoever!'

'Francesca! This isn't like you. You're usually so positive. You made a mistake and you put it right; now you're free to start again. You'll be head over heels in love again before you know it.'

Her eyes bleak, she said, 'I don't trust love any more. I thought I was in love when I was in college, but the guy just walked out of my life without a word.' She felt Calum's arm tighten around her and gave him a wan smile. 'Then I thought I was in love with Paolo. It seemed like a fairy-tale, falling in love with the handsome prince, but the magic didn't last. He turned the palace into a prison, and our bedroom into a torture-chamber.' She gave a mirthless laugh. 'The dream became a nightmare, and sometimes I thought I'd never wake up, never be free of him. I longed to be divorced so that I could start living again, but now that I am free I'm still not happy. I don't know what to do, Calum.' She looked up at her cousin pleadingly. 'Tell me what to do.'

There was a rather grim look around Calum's mouth, but he said, 'All right—but give me a little time to think about it. Then we'll talk some more, perhaps when this week is over and we have more time.' Drawing her to him, he kissed her forehead. 'I want you to promise me that for this week, for Grandfather's sake, you'll try and enjoy yourself. You know how he dotes on you; he wouldn't want to see you at all unhappy.'

'I know. And I do try.'

'You're a good, brave girl.' He glanced up and released her. 'Here's Elaine looking for you again.' Straightening, he glanced at his watch. 'I think I'll go and check on Grandfather. See you at dinner.'

He left them. Francesca made a phone call for Elaine because it involved speaking Portuguese, and was left on her own again. She wondered how Chris was getting on with Tiffany, and felt renewed anger at the girl's effrontery in pushing her way uninvited into their house, their lives. She wondered if that episode when she had slapped Sam Gallagher's face had been a ploy cooked up between the two of them, but then decided that it couldn't have been. Thoughtfully, she picked up the phone and began to call the hotels in Oporto, asking if Sam Gallagher was staying there. She found him at the Porto Atlantico, one of the best hotels in town, which somewhat surprised her; she hadn't put him down as living in that kind of style.

The operator at the hotel gave her Sam's room number and asked if she wanted the call put through to him, but Francesca decided not to speak to him at the moment. Maybe it would be better to wait and see how things went tonight. After all, she still had no proof that Tiffany was a gatecrasher; she just might have had an invitation passed on to her. Moodily, Francesca went up to change for dinner, already regretting the impulse that had made her ask Tiffany to stay to the meal. But then, she seemed to be doing a lot of things she regretted lately, Michel being one of them.

Nearly everyone had arrived before Tiffany put in an appearance that night. Francesca, in a silver sheath dress, was with Chris and Calum in the hall, greeting the last arrivals, when Tiffany came down the stairs to join them. But those were hardly the words to describe it: she definitely and deliberately timed her entrance on the scene to create the best effect. She stood at the top of the stairs, admittedly looking stunning in the black velvet dress, and waited until she had attracted Chris and Calum's notice, then stayed where she was for a while longer, to savour the moment, before coming down to join them.

They all went into the drawing-room for pre-dinner drinks. Although she hadn't any proof, Francesca was convinced in her own mind that Tiffany was an interloper; the idea preyed on her mind and she found it difficult to hide her feelings completely. But she tried to be fair, not knowing Tiffany's circumstances, so decided to warn her off by saying, almost as if it were just social conversation, 'Isn't it strange that Lennox is the only one—so far—of the younger generation of Brodeys to have married a blonde? Perhaps Chris and Calum are bored with all the hype the tradition has been given and with blondes of every shade continually chasing after them. I think they ought to break with it. Don't you agree?'

To her surprise, Tiffany didn't look at all embarrassed or annoyed. She said, 'Oh, absolutely,' as if she really meant it, and went on, 'How dated to let oneself be ruled by a family habit, especially when it comes to falling in love. Tell me, are there any traditions governing whom the women of your family can marry?'

Sensing that she was about to be attacked, Francesca looked at her warily and said, 'Oh, no. We're quite free to pick and choose.'

'Oh, that's good. I quite thought you had to start at the top of the aristocratic tree and work your way down.'

Not just an attack but full-scale war, Francesca realised. Well, she'd see who'd win the battle! But she had to admit that she rather admired Tiffany for that thrust; maybe she was more than just a cheap little gold-digger, after all.

It occurred to her that she could pay her back for that taunt and do herself a favour as well, so she slipped into the dining-room and switched round a couple of place-cards. Chris had told her to put him next to Tiffany but she put his card next to her own, near the centre of the table, and moved Michel's next to that of Tiffany, at the end near the door.

Michel would be extremely annoyed, not only that he was no longer next to her, but also at being at the end of the table. Her mother, as Grandfather's only daughter, was nominally the hostess tonight and liked to sit in the centre of the long table, opposite Grandfather, and Michel's rank warranted a place next to her. As rank was about all Michel had left, he guarded it carefully, and he would be bound to guess that it was she, Francesca, who had slighted him like this. Well, OK; if he felt so insulted that he left and went home, so much the better. It would save her having to tell him right out that she didn't care for him.

Chris was annoyed when he found out what she'd done and had no hesitation in telling her so. But Francesca was unrepentant, and was rather amused to see both Tiffany and Michel immediately start a flirtation, giving each other all their attention, Michel with the very obvious intention of making her jealous. Francesca couldn't have cared less and was in no way jealous, but it rather surprised her to see that Chris was.

After dinner, as they left the dining-room, Francesca was behind Tiffany and noticed that she was carrying just a very small evening-bag; she must have left her handbag upstairs in the room she'd been using. The invitations which had been sent out for the garden-party

that afternoon had been embossed on to a large, stiff
card, much too big to go into that little purse, even if
folded in half. So Tiffany's invitation must still be in
her other bag—if she'd received one. Impulsively,
Francesca excused herself and ran up to the guest room,
slipped inside and turned on the light.

Tiffany's bag was standing on the dressing-table.
Francesca hesitated for a moment, knowing this was
wrong, shameful even. But she just *had* to know.
Fighting her conscience, she picked up the bag and
looked inside. There were a few items of make-up in it,
but no address book or diary, no letters or anything with
Tiffany's name and address on it, and definitely no invitation. To make absolutely sure, Francesca looked
around the room and in the waste-paper baskets there
and in the bathroom. Nothing. She'd been right: Tiffany
was the gatecrasher!

Downstairs again, she found Michel waiting for her
in the hall. Without preamble he said, 'I suppose you
found it amusing to have me sit next to that girl?'

'Yes, I did rather,' Francesca returned. 'I hope you
found it equally amusing to flirt with the poor thing all
evening.'

Michel pounced on that with some satisfaction.
'Tiffany is a charming girl. Why shouldn't I be attentive
to her, especially when——?'

'No reason at all,' Francesca broke in. 'I'm glad you
were. It proved to me what kind of man you are, and
makes it easier for me to say that I don't want to see
you again.'

He stared at her. 'You don't mean that.'

'I'm sorry. I'm afraid I do.'

Spreading his hands in an angry Gallic gesture, he said,
'Pah! You are just trying to test me, because you're angry

that I gave the girl a little attention. You know I don't care about her. You know you're the only one for me. So beautiful, so——'

'So rich,' Francesca finished for him. 'Sorry, Michel, but I'm not interested.'

She went to walk past him but he caught her arm. 'You do not mean just money to me; surely you know that?'

Looking into his eyes, Francesca saw that he was sincere. 'Perhaps not,' she acknowledged. 'But I'm sorry, Michel; it's time to move on.'

'But you have invited me here for the whole week.'

She shrugged. 'Stay, then, if you want to.'

'You are only doing this to punish me,' he said angrily, unable and unwilling to believe that she meant what she said.

Francesca was about to tell him very definitely that she meant it, but the door to the drawing-room opened, and Lennox and Stella came out, about to leave. The day had been a long one, and the other guests followed them out, saying general goodbyes. Angry with Michel, and wanting to annoy Tiffany, Francesca decided to kill two birds with one stone. Going up to Tiffany, who was obviously waiting for someone to offer her a ride, she said, 'Michel is going into Oporto, Tiffany. He can take you home. I'm sure you'll find something terribly amusing to talk about on the way.'

But Calum intervened and insisted on taking Tiffany himself. He sent for his chauffeur and the car, and helped Tiffany into it in front of them all. Francesca, though, didn't wait to see. Determined to prove her suspicions, and curious to find out where Tiffany lived, she slipped round to the garage and got out her own car, then drove down the tradesmen's entrance and along the road to

the outskirts of Oporto. There she stopped and, taking
out her mobile phone, she called Calum's car.

When he answered she made out that she was still at
the house and told him that Tiffany had left her clothes
behind. 'Ask her to come and collect them tomorrow
afternoon, about three.'

Calum's large limo came along soon afterwards and
Francesca followed it the rest of the way. Luckily, there
wasn't too much traffic about and she was able to hang
back, then stop as she saw Calum's car pull up outside
one of the better apartment blocks. He took Tiffany
inside but didn't stay, driving away shortly afterwards.
Feeling rather disappointed, Francesca was about to leave
herself when, to her surprise and excitement, she saw
Tiffany look furtively out of the door and then come
out into the street again and walk away.

Quickly, Francesca locked the car and followed her,
keeping well back. Tiffany went through some side-streets
that led to a much less affluent quarter of the city, then
down a cobbled unlit court which smelled of cats and
rotting rubbish. In one of the tall houses which ranged
around it, there was a lighted window. Watching from
the shadows, Francesca saw Tiffany pick up some
pebbles and throw them up at the pane, the noise as they
hit the glass loud in the darkness. The window opened,
a girl looked out and dropped something down to her.
A key, Francesca guessed, because Tiffany walked round
to a door with the words Pensão Brasil over it, indi-
cating that it was a cheap lodging-house, and quietly let
herself in. After a while the light at the window went
out, so Francesca turned and walked back to the car.

It was a short drive to the Porto Atlantico. Knowing
Sam's room number, Francesca was able to walk straight
over to the lifts and go up to his floor. It was late, almost

one in the morning, but she had no hesitation in
knocking on his door. She had to repeat the knock loudly
before he called out, 'Who is it?'

'Francesca de Vieira. We met this afternoon.'

Sam opened the door, his hair dishevelled, a blue
towelling robe tied round his waist, his legs bare under-
neath. Most men seemed to shrink without their outdoor
clothes, but Sam had the opposite effect—he seemed
taller and broader in just the robe.

'Did I wake you?' Francesca said in surprise. 'I'm so
sorry.' And she walked past him into the room.

Sam stayed by the open door, an incredulous, wary
look in his eyes. 'Look, Princess, I don't know why
you're here, but——'

'But that's what I came to tell you,' Francesca said
with a smile, dropping her jacket on to a chair.

It was the sitting-room of a suite, large and modern,
with a couple of good pictures on the walls. Through
an open door she could see the bedroom, the covers
pushed back, a room that seemed to have a prepon-
derance of mirrors.

'I've never been in this hotel before,' she remarked.
'Is it comfortable?'

'Very.' Sam closed the door and turned to face her,
running a hand through his hair to straighten it. 'Didn't
it occur to you to phone before you came up here?'

Francesca's brows rose. 'No. Why should I?'

Sam shook his head in disbelief. 'What do you want,
Princess?'

Francesca was sure that Sam had been tricked by
Tiffany as they had been, but she didn't come right out
and say it; she wanted Sam to admit it himself first. So,
watching him closely, she let her face fill with contrite
concern that wasn't all play-acting, and said, 'I've come

here on behalf of my family to offer you our apologies, Mr Gallagher. We really are very sorry that you were asked to leave like that, but, you see, at the time we had no idea that Tiffany Dean was a gatecrasher. We rather naturally thought that she had taken offence at something you'd said to her. It was only later we found that she'd invented the whole incident,' she added firmly, her voice carrying all the conviction of someone absolutely sure of her facts.

She waited, holding her breath, and gave an inner sigh of relief when Sam shrugged and said reluctantly, 'Yes, well, I suppose she had good reason. I hope you didn't throw *her* out right in front of everyone?'

'Oh, no, of course not. But it must have been terribly embarrassing for you, Mr Gallagher. Tell me, why did you go along with it? If you'd denied it...'

'I felt sorry for Tiffany,' Sam said bluntly. 'She seemed a nice girl, even though she did crash the party.'

'She told you that?'

'Not in so many words. But it was pretty obvious. Say, how did——?'

'You could even forgive her for slapping your face?' Francesca broke in jokingly. Sam's robe had loosened a little and she could see his bare chest, deeply tanned and with a mat of hairs. Ordinarily Francesca found hairy chests a turn-off, but Sam was so broad and strong that somehow it seemed right on him. Deep inside, hunger stirred, and she realised how long it was since she'd been with a man.

Sam grinned. 'I've had plenty worse. How did you find out about Tiffany?'

Licking lips gone dry, Francesca gave a light laugh. 'Well, it's quite a long story, and I don't want to keep you up. How about if you come out to the house again tomorrow and I'll tell you all about it?'

'Well, I don't know...'

She gave him an appealing look and moved nearer to put a hand on his arm, her eyes pleading. 'I really would like you to come, Mr Gallagher—Sam. That's if you're not too busy...'

It was a look that few men had been able to resist, and Sam was no exception. 'No—I guess I can make that.'

'Great. Shall we say about three?'

'OK, I'll be there.'

She picked up her jacket and he came to hold it for her, his hand momentarily brushing hers. Again she felt a stirring of desire, which was ridiculous in these circumstances and with this man.

Sam went to open the door for her, but said, 'Why did you come yourself? You could have phoned.'

'We were all so upset by the injustice we'd done you,' Francesca murmured. 'I just had to come.'

'But why you and not one of your cousins?'

She waved an airy hand. 'Our house guests, you know. Goodnight, Mr Gallagher. Until tomorrow.'

Driving home, Francesca smiled with satisfaction at the success of her ploy. Tomorrow would be interesting, and she realised with faint surprise that it also might be interesting to meet Sam again.

Calum knew that Tiffany was coming the next afternoon, of course—he'd even sent a car for her, but Francesca made sure that Chris was also in the room when Tiffany arrived. Tiffany was early, which was annoying; Francesca would have liked to see her face when confronted with Sam. As it was she had to make small talk while she waited for Sam to arrive. As she'd lain in bed last night, Francesca's conscience had troubled her a little, and she had thought of telling Calum what she had found out. Now she was glad she hadn't: Tiffany had walked in as if she had every right to be there, and the way she was smiling at Calum was almost nauseating. Seeing her cousin so taken in made Francesca's anger grow; Tiffany was a liar and a cheat and she deserved everything that was coming to her.

The maid brought in the coffee-tray and Calum went to pour it out, giving Francesca a smile, because he knew she objected to being expected to do domestic things like that just because she happened to be female. It was then that Sam was shown into the room.

A dark frown of outrage came into Calum's face, but, before he could speak, Francesca quickly went to welcome Sam.

'Mr Gallagher. Thank you so much for coming. We wanted to——'

But Sam noticed Tiffany and saw her face whiten in alarm. 'What is this?' he demanded.

'Yes.' Calum gave Francesca a grim look. 'Just what *is* Mr Gallagher doing here, Francesca?'

She waited until the maid had closed the door, holding them all in suspense for those few long moments. Then, looking at Calum, she said, 'I asked him to come here because our family has done him an injustice and we owe him an apology.'

Sam took a hasty step forward. 'That wasn't why I came here——'

But Calum, his eyes fixed on her grimly, said, 'And just why does he deserve an apology from us? Surely it should be the other way round? It was he who abused our hospitality by his boorish behaviour to one of our guests.'

Tiffany's face went even whiter and she made a strangled protest, knowing from Francesca's resolute face what was coming.

For a second Francesca felt a pang of pity, but buried it as she told them that Tiffany had gatecrashed the garden-party.

She started to explain how she'd found out, but Chris said sharply, 'Leave this, Francesca. Let it go.'

'But that wouldn't be fair,' she protested. 'And nor was the way we treated Mr Gallagher.' She told them how she'd tracked Sam down and he'd admitted the truth. 'He accepted the situation because he didn't want to get Tiffany into trouble——'

There was anger in Sam's voice as he interrupted, 'That wasn't how I remember it went. As far as I'm concerned that incident was closed yesterday. And I don't like the way you're doing this, Princess,' he added grimly.

He turned to go but Calum stopped him. 'Just one moment. I think we need to get to the bottom of this.' Turning to Tiffany, he meant to ask her for the truth, but she cut across him and admitted everything before he could do so. But she didn't do it abjectly, as most people found out like that would have; instead her head came up and she seemed almost proud of what she'd done. The only thing she apologised for was lying about Sam. She even had the nerve to smile at Calum and tell him she'd only done it so that she could meet him.

But the smile was lost on Calum, who, annoyed at being taken in by a cheap trick, spoke to her angrily, accusing her of scheming and lying. Chris stood by grimly, his hands thrust into his pockets as he watched them, silent now. Francesca watched too, thinking that

she ought to have been pleased that Tiffany was being
shown up like this, that she was getting what she deserved, but there was something in the other girl's de-
meanour, an unexpected dignity, that somehow made
her feel extremely embarrassed and, annoyingly, guilty
herself.

Suddenly, Tiffany turned on them like a cornered
animal. She threw their ancestry and their wealth in their
faces. Her eyes full of furious contempt, she cried out,
'You're all nothing but rich, spoilt parasites. Especially
you!' And she jerked her arm, pointing her finger at
Francesca. 'I hope the Count has more sense than to
marry you, because he's too darn good for you. Just as
I'm too good for you!' she finished haughtily, glaring
at Calum.

Her outburst stunned them all, until Francesca, indignant on her cousins' behalf, said, 'Well, really! Of
all the nerve. It was you who——'

But Calum intervened, as he apologised to Sam.

'I didn't ask for any apology and I don't want it,' Sam
cut in, and added, to Francesca's surprise, 'Tiffany, wait
for me outside. I'll take you back to town.' Then he
turned and gave Francesca a look of such grim purpose
that she took an involuntary step away from him. 'But
first I want a word with the Princess!' Striding forward,
he caught hold of Francesca's wrist and pulled her after
him through the French windows on to the terrace.

'Mr Gallagher, please!'

He took no notice of her but pulled her down the
terrace steps into the garden and across the lawn towards the shrubbery.

Angry at being dragged along like this, Francesca tried
to stop, pulling back against his grip, but she might just
as well not have bothered for all the difference it made.

His grip was like steel and his strength so great that to resist him was impossible. Becoming more annoyed by the minute, she yelled, 'Hey!' and he finally came to a stop behind a tall, wide-spreading bush, its shadow black across the garden. But he had stopped because that was where he wanted to be, hidden from the house, not because she'd yelled at him.

'Really, Mr Gallagher,' Francesca said indignantly, struggling to keep her temper. 'There was no need to——'

'There was every need,' he retorted. 'Just what kind of person are you, Princess? Did it give you a buzz to kick Tiffany in the teeth like that? Did it ever occur to you, *Princess*, to wonder just why she did it?'

'You have no reason to speak to me like this, Mr Gallagher. And stop calling me "Princess", as if it's some kind of dirty word.'

'OK, so we'll drop the titles. I'm Sam, you're Francesca. Just ordinary people, human beings. Just as Tiffany is an ordinary——'

'Oh, no,' she cut in swiftly. 'Tiffany is an impostor; she admitted that herself. She had no right to come here and——'

'And you had no right to expose her like that. You brought her here this afternoon just to rub her nose in the dirt. *And* you enjoyed it!'

'I wanted Calum to see her for what she is. He has a right to know,' she said stiffly.

'So why didn't you just tell him?' Sam's face grew grim. 'It seems to me you're a cruel, sadistic bitch!'

Francesca gasped, unable to believe her ears. Instinctively, she turned to march away, but forgot that Sam still had hold of her wrist.

Jerking her back, he said, 'Oh, no, I haven't finished with you yet. OK, so Tiffany tried her luck at the party yesterday. What the hell's so almighty terrible about that? She didn't do any harm to anyone.'

'Except you,' Francesca said quickly. 'She not only hurt you physically, but she also hurt your reputation. I couldn't allow one of our guests to be treated like that. She had to be made to apologise to you.'

'Bullshit!' Sam exploded, making her gasp again. 'You couldn't care less about my feelings. You just like being the centre of attention so much that you got jealous when Tiffany threatened to steal the limelight, when she started getting your cousins' attention.'

'That isn't true,' Francesca returned hotly. 'And just who the hell do you think you are, speaking to me like this? I think you'd better leave—and take that gate-crashing little liar you seem to be so keen on with you!'

'It'll be a pleasure,' Sam returned, his jaw hardening. 'This is my first brush with the aristocracy, and if you're anything to go by, then I certainly don't want to meet any more.'

Francesca drew herself up to her full height, wishing she could tower over this man as she did with so many others, but finding that he was still taller than she was. Her grey eyes alight with fury, she said scathingly, 'Now I come to think of it, you weren't personally invited to our party either. So no wonder you're defending that little tramp—you're just as much of a free-loader as she is!'

Sam's hand tightened on her wrist, the fingers bruising her flesh. A murderous gleam came into his eyes and he said, 'Just watch it, Princess. If you were a man you'd be flat on your back by now. And your being a woman ain't gonna stop me from putting you across my knee if you make one more crack like that.'

'Why, you—you cowboy!' Francesca exclaimed furiously.

'Yeah, that's right. I am a cowboy. And proud of it,' he answered, his square jaw jutting forward.

'Let go of me! Let go or I'll scream for Chris and Calum.'

But he ignored her, saying, 'You owe Tiffany an apology for what you did today.'

She gave an outraged gasp. 'Well, I'm certainly not going to make one.'

Francesca expected him to threaten her again at that, but was surprised to find that Sam merely gave her a contemplative look that changed to a slow smile she didn't like. 'Oh, but I think you will.' Letting go of her wrist, he began to walk away, but then turned and said, again making it an insult, 'So long—*Princess*.'

Francesca watched him go, rubbing her wrist in helpless anger. It was obvious that he was as attracted to Tiffany as Chris and Calum had been. Well, let him take her and go, get out of their lives. They deserved each other!

But when she got to the house she heard the maid telling Sam that Tiffany had been taken home in Calum's car. Now he would have to search for her, she realised. And she remembered in the same moment that she was the only one who knew where Tiffany really lived. Angry and vengeful against them both, Francesca looked up the number of the Pensão Brasil, rang it, and asked the landlord if she could speak to Senhora Tiffany Dean. When he denied that anyone of that name was staying there, she gave him the interesting information that he, too, had a gatecrasher on the premises.

CHAPTER THREE

THAT evening the whole family were going to the Brodey wine lodge in Vila Nova de Gaia, where Old Calum was to take the first drink from a pipe of port, laid down years ago in anticipation of the bicentenary. They were to be joined at the little ceremony by all the Brodey staff who worked in Oporto and their families, together with some other guests from the city: staff from the bank they used, from the shipping company, the barrel-makers, the label-printers, all the companies who depended to a great extent on their business and who had served them well over the years. Afterwards, they were all to dine at the cellar.

Knowing the coolness of the cellar, Francesca put on black evening trousers and a sequinned black sweater. She was ready quite early and went down to the sitting-room to wait for the others. Pouring herself a drink, she turned as the maid showed Michel into the room. So much had happened today that Francesca had almost forgotten the way she'd rebuffed him the previous evening. In fact, she'd hardly given him a thought today, which just went to prove that she didn't care about him enough to marry him.

But Michel, it seemed, was intent on making up their quarrel. Coming straight across to her, he picked up her hand to kiss it. 'How beautiful you look. And how lucky that I should find you alone. Francesca, *chérie*, I——'

'What would you like to drink?' He was still holding her hand and she pulled it free.

But he wasn't to be put off so easily. Capturing both her hands, he held them firmly. 'You are still angry with me, I see. But how do you expect me to react when you are so cruel to me?'

She went to speak, to deny that she'd been anything of the sort, but then Francesca remembered the accusation that Tiffany had thrown at her, telling her that Michel was too good for her. It had just been petty spite, of course, but even so it made her hesitate for a fraction too long and Michel, encouraged by it, went on, 'Sometimes I think you play with me, my beautiful Francesca. And sometimes I think you are afraid, too. You have had one bad experience; I understand that. But surely you must know that I love you far too much ever to hurt you in any way? To me you are the most——'

'Michel, please!'

This time she had to interrupt, but he caught her to him and gave her a look of adoration. 'No, I will make you listen to me. You will hear how much I love you, how much I want and desire you.' And, despite her indignant protest, he bent her back to kiss her.

It was inevitable that someone should walk into the room. There was a giggle from the maid and a masculine cough. Michel didn't seem to hear but, using all her strength, Francesca managed to push him away. She expected to see a member of the family, but her face flamed when she saw that Sam Gallagher had been shown in. He was watching them with a grin on his face, half of mockery, half of scorn.

'Sorry to interrupt,' he said sardonically. 'I wanted to speak to your cousin.'

'To Calum?' Francesca's tone was curt; she was furious with Sam for having caught her in such a situation—that he of all people had seen her in that unwanted em-

brace. She was even more furious with Michel for putting
her in it.

'Yes.'

'He isn't down yet.'

'Maybe there's someplace else I could wait?' Sam said,
the mockery uppermost now.

'That won't be necessary,' she answered stiffly. 'I'll
go and find him for you.'

'The maid's already gone.'

Michel, angry at the interruption for an entirely different reason, had gone to pour himself a drink, his back
expressive of his annoyance.

'Perhaps you could fix a drink for Mr Gallagher?'
Francesca said to him.

'Oh, yes—Mr—er—Gallagher. What would you like?'

Michel pretended he'd forgotten Sam, but Francesca
knew he hadn't; Sam was so tall and broad, had such
presence despite his casual air, that he would be a difficult person for anyone to forget. Seeing him reminded
Francesca of the *frisson* of sensuality he'd roused in her
last night, but she put that firmly out of her mind.

'Guess I'll have Scotch on the rocks.'

Francesca, her poise recovered, went to sit on a sofa,
her arms spread along the back. 'What brings you back
here so soon, Mr Gallagher? I thought you were never
going to darken our door again.'

'The name's Sam.'

'Of course. Sam. I beg your pardon.'

Sam took his drink from Michel and gave Francesca
a contemplative look, having recognised the challenge
in her tone. 'A personal matter,' he answered shortly.

Her left eyebrow rising, Francesca said, 'Is that supposed to put me off?'

But he was a match for that, saying, 'It was a polite way of telling you to mind your own business, yes.'

'Calum has no secrets from me.'

'Then Calum's a fool,' Sam returned shortly.

'Am I?' Calum walked into the room in time to hear. 'Hello, Mr Gallagher.'

'Sam,' Sam said automatically as he turned to shake Calum's hand.

'Why am I a fool?'

'He thinks you ought to keep secrets from me,' Francesca told him, smiling confidently, sure that he never would.

But the startled look that came into Calum's eyes held the smile fixed to her face. Calum laughed, the sound not quite natural. 'Of course I have secrets from you. What man wouldn't?'

She smiled uncertainly, glanced at Sam and saw that he too had seen, and was amused by it. Her trust in her cousin meant a great deal to Francesca, and for a moment the trust slipped. Suddenly afraid that this too might be taken away from her, and furious with Sam for just being there and seeing it, she said spitefully, '*Sam,*' saying it exactly the same way as he had emphasised 'Princess' earlier that afternoon, 'has a secret he wants to discuss with you. I doubt, though, that it's of much importance: little men very seldom have big secrets.'

Calum blinked, but Sam didn't look at all disconcerted by this thrust. He merely squared his broad shoulders, raised an eyebrow, and said, 'Little?'

'I meant in the worldly sense, not the physical,' Francesca explained sarcastically. 'But I should have realised you wouldn't understand.'

Sam gave a grim smile and looked as if he was going to make a scathing comment, but Calum hastily interrupted. 'Will it take long, Sam? I'm afraid we're all due to have dinner at the wine-lodge. I'm sure that——'

He broke off as there was the sound of voices outside and then the door was opened and old Mr Brodey, together with several members of the family, came in. It was impossible to talk privately then, and Calum was ordered by his grandfather to pour drinks, so he couldn't leave. Old Calum, becoming aware that there was a stranger in the room, greeted Sam affably and took it for granted that he was going with them to the lodge.

'Why, no, sir.' Sam started to excuse himself and said to Calum. 'I'll come back tomorrow.'

'I probably won't be here. Look, why don't you come with us to the lodge? I'll find some time to talk to you there.'

Sam hesitated, then agreed. But he did it rather reluctantly, Francesca noticed. Still angry, she got up and went to help Calum with the drinks. 'Did you have to ask him?' she hissed at him.

'It's the least I could do—especially after throwing him out of the garden-party by mistake. Why, don't you like him?'

'No, I don't,' she said definitely. 'Promise me you'll tell me what he wants to see you about.'

'Francesca!'

'Promise,' she whispered fiercely.

He gave her an exasperated look. 'Oh, all right. Here, take this G and T to your mother.'

There was a whole fleet of cars waiting to take the family into town. Sam and Michel both had their own cars, and Michel confidently held open the passenger door of his big silver-grey Mercedes that he'd driven down from France, waiting for Francesca who had gone back for her bag. Sam, coming out of the house with the others, said to Calum, 'I don't know where the lodge is; maybe you could come with me and show me the way, then we could talk?'

'Unfortunately I have to drive one of the other cars. I'll get someone else to direct you.' He looked round but most of the family were already sorting themselves out. Then Francesca came running to join them. Perhaps getting his own back, Calum said, 'Francesca knows the way; she'll show you.'

Francesca immediately opened her mouth to object, saw Michel waiting for her and changed her mind, saying meekly, 'Yes, of course. Is this your car, Sam?'

She got in the passenger side of the plain hired car and pulled the door firmly closed. Sam, his mouth quirked in amusement, got in beside her. Michel started to walk towards them, but she said, 'Don't just sit there—go!'

Sam, infuriatingly, said, 'Maybe Michel wants to come with us.'

'Not in this car, he won't,' Francesca said with certainty.

But Sam wound down his window. 'Francesca's going to show me the way,' he told Michel. 'Why not come with us?'

For a moment the Count was torn, but then he gave a very French shrug. 'No, I'll need my car later; I will follow you.'

'See you there, then.' Sam closed the window and glanced at Francesca. 'It seems you were right.'

'That car is his pride and joy; he wouldn't be seen dead in anything else.'

'Not even to be with you?'

She gave him a sharp glance, then said lightly, 'Don't all men put their cars before their women?'

'Not in the States, they don't.'

'A great many in Europe do.'

'I suppose it depends on the woman in a man's life,' Sam said thoughtfully.

'Not the car?'

'Oh, a car will always respond if you treat it right.'

'So will a woman, I imagine,' Francesca said wryly.

That made him grin. 'Maybe Americans know how to treat their women better than Europeans do.'

'Maybe most Americans are scared to death of their wives,' Francesca rejoined tartly.

Sam laughed. 'Not in Wyoming, they're not.'

She gave him a contemplative look. 'You think you're very macho, don't you?'

'Is that how I come across to you?' he asked with a slight frown.

'Oh, no. To me you seem to be just a common-or-garden chauvinist. Rather boorish, but otherwise typical of the breed.'

'And there was I beginning to think you'd fallen for my undoubted charm,' Sam remarked, in no way put out. 'Which way at the lights?'

'Left.' Francesca fought an inclination to be amused and said, 'What charm?'

The lights turned to red and Sam was able to look at her. 'What's with you and Michel? One minute you're kissing him, the next you're trying to avoid him. Do you always play those kind of games with men?'

Her face tightened and Francesca ignored the question, instead saying, 'What did you want to see Calum about?'

'Why are you so interested?'

'You and Calum have only one thing in common.'

Sam put the car into gear as the lights became green. 'And that is?'

'Tiffany Dean, of course. Are you looking for her?'

'Do you know where she is?'

'So you *are* looking for her. Why?'

'Why do you think?' he countered.

'Because you're attracted to her too, I suppose.'

Francesca looked contemplatively out of the window, wondering what it was about Tiffany that had interested the three men: Calum, Chris, and now Sam. All three of them were tall, of course, so maybe it was the attraction of opposites; perhaps they were intrigued by Tiffany's shortness and her air of fragility, like a china doll. Perhaps she had aroused their protective instincts—something she, Francesca, had never done, she thought resentfully.

But no, that wasn't completely true: her grandfather was protective, and so were her cousins, to a degree. But then, they knew her very well. Ordinary men tended to be overawed, initially by her height and beauty, and then by her supreme sophistication and air of self-confident independence. To some of them, of course, it was a turn-on, a challenge, but there were few who could meet her on equal terms. And Michel wasn't one of them. He had caught her on the rebound from that terrible divorce and had taken full advantage of her weakness, but she was recovering now and knew that she couldn't tolerate him for much longer. Francesca supposed that he had been kind in his way, so she would try and break off the relationship gently, without denting his pride too much.

'Who else is attracted to Tiffany?' Sam was asking her.

'Calum. Chris.'

'But Calum was furious with her this afternoon, after you staged your big denouncement scene.'

Francesca shot him an angry look. 'He doesn't like being made a fool of—but evidently you don't care, because she certainly made a fool out of you!'

Sam shrugged. 'It didn't bother me.'

'It ought to have done. How could you possibly let yourself be thrown out and let her get away with it?'

'She looked as if she needed help.'

Francesca remembered the look that Tiffany had given Sam at the time, her blue eyes large and pleading, and perhaps a little frightened. Was Sam basically kind, then, or just a sucker for a pretty face? Rather angrily, she said, 'She's just a cheap little confidence trickster. I'm glad I found out what she was.'

'So are you a confidence trickster,' Sam said shortly. 'You deceived me when you came to my hotel, made me admit the truth. You're no better than she is, Francesca— Probably worse, because Tiffany must have had good reason to do what she did. She was probably desperate. You don't even know the meaning of the word.'

'The wine-lodge is down the next turning to the right,' she said curtly. 'That's the building, with the lights outside.' Sam pulled up and Francesca went to open the door, but turned a set face towards him and said, 'Thank you so much for the lift. Being with you is always a lesson in boorish behaviour.' And then, driven by some inner compulsion, she added with deep bitterness, 'And you're quite wrong; I know all there is to know about desperation.' Getting out of the car, she slammed the door and strode through the lodge gates without looking back.

They waited in the small, flower-filled courtyard until all the family had arrived, then old Calum Brodey led

the way into the big tasting-room where all the lodge
staff were gathered. He was greeted by the senior em-
ployees, many of whom had worked for Brodey's for
several years, and then made a ceremony of it, going
round the room shaking hands with everyone there. He
was followed by his three grandsons, all of whom worked
for the company. His two surviving children and
Francesca stood back; their shares in the company earned
them a great deal of money, but they took no part in
the running of the business.

Francesca watched the four men a little wistfully,
thinking that if she'd been born a male she would have
been there with them now, would have had some purpose
in her life, work to do, goals to achieve.

She felt someone watching her and glanced to her
right. It was Sam, gazing at her with a thoughtful look
in his lazy brown eyes. Her chin came up, and she was
annoyed with herself for having given something of
herself away to him earlier. But he had made her angry,
going on about how desperate Tiffany must have been.
It had all been Tiffany, Tiffany, until she'd had to let
him know that she was just as capable of despair, just
as vulnerable. Which had been a big mistake, of course.
And why she'd been stupid enough to do it she couldn't
think. After all, what the hell did it matter what the Sam
Gallaghers of this world thought of her? He was no one,
a stranger passing momentarily through their lives, of
no importance whatsoever.

After the men had shaken hands with all their em-
ployees and guests, drinks were handed out, a speech of
congratulations was made by the senior member of staff
and Old Calum replied on behalf of the family. He made
several jokes, and the mood was happy and convivial.
Then he led the way into the vast wine cellar.

It wasn't a real cellar because it wasn't below ground,
and resembled, more than anything, a huge wooden
hangar. The building was very old, the timbers black
with age and festooned with cobwebs. Great wooden
casks stood on stones that lifted them off the ground;
they stood in rows, the air heavy with the sweet smell
of the maturing port. Against the outside walls smaller
casks lay on their sides, each one marked with the date
when it had been filled, the type of port, and the name
'BRODEY' stamped into the wood, each of them holding
a pipe of wine.

Beyond this huge cellar there were other darker rooms
where the bottled vintage wines were quietly ageing, but
even there there was not much light, the floors were dusty
and the air cool.

Cálum was walking with Sam, explaining the wine-
making process to him. They all reached the celebration
cask and Old Calum gave another short speech, prom-
ising everyone a special souvenir bottle of the wine,
before ceremoniously turning the tap that had been let
into it. A cheer went up as the tawny liquid poured into
the waiting utensil. Old Calum tasted it carefully, a lifetime's experience in his palate, while everyone waited
anxiously, then he smiled and declared it eminently
drinkable.

Glasses of the port were handed round, toasts were
drunk, and there was a lot of laughter and cheering.
More wine was poured and the conversation became
general for a while. Sam took the opportunity to talk to
Calum, standing with him towards the back of the crowd.

Chris noticed them and went over to Francesca. 'What
does Sam Gallagher want?'

'I don't know; he wouldn't tell me.'

Chris raised an eyebrow. 'Couldn't you persuade him?'

She gave a small shrug. 'He and I haven't exactly hit if off.'

'Why not?'

'He didn't like it when I exposed Tiffany Dean as an impostor.'

'I didn't like the way you did it either. And it was completely unnecessary; Calum would have realised for himself soon enough.'

Francesca gave him a quick glance, half antagonistic, half appealing. 'You're not going to turn against me as well, are you?'

Chris put an arm round her shoulders. 'No. You know I never would. But you shouldn't take your unhappiness out on other people.'

'Is that what I was doing?' she said with a short laugh. 'I didn't know; I really thought I was saving us from a gold-digging impostor.'

Breaking away from him, Francesca walked over to join her grandfather as everyone walked through to an adjoining cellar. Here, again under Elaine Beresford's supervision, long tables had been set out for dinner in the aisle between the casks. There were scarlet tablecloths, candles, and brightly lit lamps hanging from temporary fittings in the roof, so that there was a blaze of colour and brilliance in that usually dark place. Crystal glass sparkled in the light, and a beautifully wrapped gift lay next to each plate. The atmosphere was one of warmth and achievement, of lives crossing and shared, of mutual respect and quiet satisfaction, and a determination to enjoy this special night.

All the speeches had, of course, been in Portuguese. Old Calum said something else in that language, and everyone laughed and moved to take their seats.

Sam happened to be near Francesca and he touched her arm. 'What did your grandfather say?'

'Oh, he just advised the men not to sit next to their own wives if they wanted to drink. Sit where you like.'

She went to turn away but he said, 'You're sure it's OK for me to stay?' He gave her a wry look. 'I'd hate to be accused of free-loading again.'

She looked amused. 'That still rankles, does it? No, Calum invited you, didn't he? So stay.'

'Are there going to be any more speeches?'

'Do you find them boring?'

'I don't find them anything—I just don't understand them. Maybe I'd better sit next to you so you can translate for me.' And he put a hand under her elbow to guide her towards two empty seats.

Hadn't the man ever thought of asking first? Francesca thought indignantly, and, pulling her arm free, she strode instead to where Michel was looking round for her and sat beside him at the long table. Sam, apparently in no way put out, came and sat almost directly opposite. Having taken a dislike to Sam, Michel immediately began to talk to Francesca in French, telling her how they always celebrated Bastille Day on his estate in Anjou in much the same way as this, everyone in the village coming to join in.

'When are you going to let me show you my château?' he said persuasively. 'You would love it there, I know.'

But Francesca refused to commit herself, saying that her plans were undecided. 'I might stay here with Grandfather for a while. He likes me to spend part of the spring with him.'

'But you should see my estate at this time of the year, *chérie*; all the fruit trees are in blossom and there are carpets of bluebells. We could——'

'Say, have you ever been to Wyoming?'

Sam's voice interrupted them and they both glanced towards him.

'No,' Michel said shortly, and turned back to Francesca. 'As I was saying, the spring flowers in the gardens are——'

'We have two of the most beautiful national parks in the world in Wyoming. I guess you must have heard of the Yellowstone?' Sam persisted.

Michel frowned in annoyance at being interrupted again. Francesca, too, frowned for a moment, but then a gleam of interest came into her eyes as she realised that Sam must be able to speak some French and had understood what Michel was saying.

'I suppose you're going to say next that this park is as big as France,' Michel said waspishly in English. 'Don't you Americans always have the biggest and the best of everything?'

'Well, I don't like to boast . . .' Sam said modestly, his eyes crinkling with laughter as he looked at Francesca, inviting her to share his amusement.

She resisted the temptation, but not without difficulty. Michel looked angry, but Sam said placatingly, 'I guess your château must be pretty old?'

'Of course. It was built in the fifteenth century.' Michel hesitated for a moment, averse to chatting with Sam, but deciding to take the opportunity to describe his house in the hope of capturing Francesca's imagination so that she would want to see it.

Sam listened with apparent attention but Francesca took little notice; she had seen the châteaux on the Loire, after which none could be as beautiful. Instead she amused herself by watching the two men and comparing them more closely. Both were tall, which was where all similarity seemed to end. Michel was lean and wiry, and his face had the high cheekbones, thin lips and lean features which were the mark of a Frenchman. He also had the suave good manners and air of innate arrogance that came from being the heir of an ancient noble family. His hands, so beautifully eloquent as he gestured when he talked, were soft and slender, with the nails professionally manicured. He had never worked a day in his life and wouldn't know how to. Looking at him under her lashes, Francesca decided that he had been born to adorn life, to live off its luxuries, to play at living and live to play. Almost an anachronism in this day and age.

But wasn't that exactly what she was herself? A grim look came into Francesca's eyes as she wondered if that was how people thought of her. The thought depressed her and she quickly looked from Michel to Sam.

Although he was a big man, Sam too was lean, all whipcord muscle and taut skin, as if he was used to getting plenty of exercise, as if he worked hard and manually. There was strength, too, in his face, in the square jaw that spoke of determination and the firm mouth that looked as if it was used to being obeyed. Only the long lashes of his brown eyes gave any gentleness to his uncompromising features. Even his hands looked strong, as if they could break someone as fragile as herself if he ever cared to exert his strength. There was nothing soft about them, and she noticed a scar that ran across the back of the left one, white against his tanned skin. She wondered what had caused the wound, whether there was someone back in Wyoming who had tended it with loving care. Whether those hands could be gentle when he made love to a woman.

She felt Sam's eyes on her and looked up quickly. He was looking at her intently, making no pretence now of listening to Michel. And there was something in his gaze, as if he'd guessed what she was thinking, that brought a slight colour to her cheeks. But she didn't lower her eyes: she was no modest, inexperienced virgin. Instead her chin came up and her grey eyes challenged him; if men could look at and think of women as sex objects, then women had every right to do the same. Though quite why she had even thought of Sam in that way Francesca had no idea. She certainly wasn't attracted to him; quite the opposite. His brusqueness and lack of finesse when they'd quarrelled that afternoon had repelled her. Maybe it was just because he was the complete opposite to all the men she knew that her imagination had been caught for a moment. Shades of Lady Chatterley and her gamekeeper!

Her challenge brought amusement to his eyes and some other emotion she couldn't fathom—approval, perhaps, although that seemed unlikely. Respect? Hardly that. So maybe it was just a simple acceptance of her challenge, picking up the invisible glove. The way his eyes continued to hold hers seemed to say so.

'Francesca!' Michel's indignant voice made her jump and turn to look at the other man. 'You are not listening to me,' he complained.

'No, I wasn't,' she said calmly. 'Were you talking to me? I thought you were telling Sam about your château.'

Caught out, Michel said shortly, 'He was not listening either.'

'Maybe he got bored. Why don't you ask him about his house?'

Michel looked taken aback, as if the house of a strange American could be of absolutely no interest to him, as if it hadn't even occurred to him to wonder about it.

But he said, 'Do you have a house in—Wyoming, Monsieur Gallagher?'

Francesca waited to hear the answer with some interest; she had suggested the question to discomfit Michel, but also to find out how Sam would react.

'The name's Sam,' Sam said patiently. 'I live in a kind of ranch-house. The same place where I work.'

'So you *are* a cowboy,' Francesca said in amusement.

'Sure.' He gave her one of his lazy grins. 'Didn't I say I was?'

'How interesting,' Michel said, meaning just the opposite. He turned to Francesca again but before he could speak someone stood up to make another speech, and she translated for both men.

The meal over, she went over to Calum. 'What did Sam want?'

'To know where Tiffany Dean lived. He seemed to feel some sort of responsibility for her. I told him she deserved nothing from him, of course. But he insisted on knowing, so I told him.'

He spoke curtly and Francesca guessed that he was still angry at the way he'd been taken in. Calum didn't like being made a fool of any more than she did. Well, Sam wouldn't find Tiffany at the address he'd been given, that was for sure. Would he give up then, she wondered, or would he go on trying to find her? The other girl had certainly made an impression on him, that was obvious, and she felt a flash of emotion that she was surprised to recognise as jealousy.

Sam thanked Old Calum for his hospitality and slipped away, to look for Tiffany presumably. Some musicians had arrived and began to play dance music in the other cellar—some traditional Portuguese tunes, some modern. They formed lines for the folk dances; the women's skirts

whirled and sent dust-motes flying up into the light of
the lamps, where they too swirled and danced. The
watchers clapped their hands and gave shouts of en-
couragement. Girls laughed in excitement, and matrons
forgot their cares and responsibilities. The men, already
flushed with wine, grew even redder in the face. A young
man, dark-haired and dark-eyed, with lean
Mediterranean good looks, boldly caught Francesca's
hand and pulled her to join in the dance.

There was little Portuguese blood in her, but Portugal
was her second home, and for the hour that she danced
Francesca was as one with the others. Her hair came
loose and flew in a golden cloud about her head; she
twisted and swayed, her slender figure outlined against
the lanterns and the candle-flames.

Finally the music stopped and musicians and dancers
alike helped themselves to much needed drinks. Flushed,
laughing, Francesca lifted a hand to push her hair back.
Across the room she saw that Sam had come back, his
search unsuccessful. He was leaning against one of the
casks, arms folded, watching her, and looking amused
by what he saw. Lifting her chin, Francesca tossed her
head in open disdain. So it amused him to see her let
her hair down, to be on a level with the workers and
their families. So what? She couldn't care less what he
felt.

Michel, though, made it plain that he didn't approve
when he called on her at the *palácio* the next morning.
He did it in a roundabout way, talking about status and
the dignity one owed to one's position in life. Realising
what he was getting at, Francesca first stared at him in
surprise, then burst into laughter.

'Well, there can be no danger of you ever losing your
dignity. I somehow can't imagine you ever lowering

yourself to mix with the workers on your estate,' she
said scathingly.

'One should keep oneself at a distance,' Michel told
her.

'How deadly boring. Michel, why don't you go back
to Paris? You're wasting your time here, you know.'

'When I am with you, my time is never wasted,' he
declared, and tried to catch her hand.

But she deftly moved out of his reach, saying, 'How
I hate fulsome remarks like that.' She turned as the door
opened. 'Oh, there you are, Elaine. I'm all ready to
leave.'

'Where are you going?' Michel wanted to know.

'To the *quinta*. We're going on ahead to prepare for
tomorrow's party.'

'You must allow me to drive you.'

'No, thanks.'

Francesca breezed out to her own sports car, Elaine
close behind her. 'Goodbye, Michel. Maybe I'll see you
around some time.' And she drove off, hoping that he
had got the message at last.

Her hope was short-lived; Michel arrived at the *quinta*
the next day with all the family and the other guests
from Oporto. But this was such a huge party that
Francesca was needed to help Elaine: to translate for
her, and make a thousand phone calls, to give orders to
men carrying tables and benches, to oversee the arrival
and cooking of food, to make sure all the drink was
under lock and key until the party began. So she had
no time to spare for Michel, and was glad of it. And
anyway, she was enjoying herself, working away under
the sunlit sky.

                          *   *   *

The party was the most successful any *quinta* had ever held—everyone said so as they picked themselves up from where they had dropped the previous night and began to straggle homeward over the steep hillside and deep valley, the sound of car engines droning off into the morning.

The members of the family pulled themselves together more slowly. All the men were there but Francesca was the only woman: her mother had called it a bacchanal feast and refused to go, and Stella, Lennox's wife, who would have loved to go, had been forced to stay at home because of her pregnancy.

Fighting headaches, they drove back to Oporto, the men having to get back in time to attend a dinner party being given in their honour that evening at the Factory House, the magnificent building erected by the port companies as their meeting house, rather like a London livery hall.

When they reached the *palácio*, Francesca went straight up to her room, changed, and went for a swim in the pool, doing a brisk crawl because the water felt cool. Afterwards she felt tired so she lay on a lounger in the conservatory attached to the pool and catnapped for a while before having a light tea. So it was quite late in the afternoon before she went up to her room again and found that a parcel had been left there for her. Unwrapping it, she found the clothes that Tiffany had chosen from the boutique: the black velvet dress and all the accessories. The shorts suit she'd left behind earlier, so Tiffany had kept nothing.

Frowning, Francesca looked down at the clothes. She certainly hadn't expected them to be returned and was disturbed that they had been. Surely gold-diggers usually kept whatever they could get their hands on? These were

good, designer clothes; even if Tiffany hadn't wanted
the things she could easily have sold them and kept the
money. But the other girl had been furiously angry after
Francesca had exposed her. So angry that she'd wanted
nothing more to do with the Brodeys and had sent the
things back out of pride? Such pride cost money; could
she afford such a grand gesture? Francesca wondered.
Somehow Francesca didn't think so. If she could, why
crash the party in the first place?

Reaching out, Francesca ran long, pearl-tipped fingers
across the black velvet. How would she have felt in the
circumstances? What would she have done? she wondered. Thrown hypocritical charity back in the giver's
face? Even if she was broke; even if it left her with
nothing? Yes, her own pride would have demanded it.
But how could she speak for a girl like Tiffany who had
used such underhand means to get to know the Brodeys?

She continued to think about it as she dressed, then,
on impulse, picked up the parcel, ran along the corridor
to Chris's room and knocked.

'Who is it?'

'Francesca.'

'You'll have to wait—I'm not dressed.'

Impatiently she opened the door and went in. Chris
was wearing just a bathrobe which he hastily drew
together. 'Francesca!' he protested.

'Oh, for heaven's sake! We used to go skinny-dipping
when we were kids. You haven't got anything I haven't
seen a hundred times.'

'A man loses all dignity when someone makes that
kind of remark. It's like a woman friend of your
mother's telling you she knew you when you were in
your pram,' Chris complained. 'What do you want?'

Dropping on to his bed, Francesca leaned back against the headboard and looked at him moodily as she gestured to the parcel. 'Tiffany sent back the clothes I gave her.'

Chris began to towel his hair dry. 'So what did you expect—a note of thanks?'

'I expected her to keep them.' She gave him a troubled look. 'Do you think she was really hard up?'

He grew still. 'Yes, I'm sure of it.'

'I don't want the wretched clothes. Can't we give them back to her?'

'We?'

'You, then. You could take them to her on your way to the dinner this evening.'

Chris shook his head. 'She isn't staying at the apartment block where Calum dropped her.'

'How do you know?'

'I went there to check a couple of days ago.'

Francesca gave a short laugh. 'You too.'

'Why, who else went there?'

'Sam Gallagher.'

'Oh, yes, Sam—of course; Calum said he'd asked for the address. They'd never heard of her there and she hasn't checked into any other hotel or boarding house in the city.'

'You've tried them all?' Francesca asked in surprise.

'Yes.' Chris went on drying his hair but there was a strained note in his voice.

She hesitated, then said slowly, 'I know where she is.'

He became still, his face sharpening. 'Where?'

'She was staying at a place called the Pensão Brasil, near the old quarter. They might not know her name, though; I think she was sharing with some other girls.'

'How do you know this?'

Standing up, Francesca said irritably, 'What does it matter how I know? Will you take the clothes back to her or not?'

'Yes, of course.'

She went downstairs to the sitting-room and poured herself a drink, wondering whether it had been a mistake to tell Chris. The phone rang and she picked up the receiver. *'Olá?'*

'Francesca? This is Sam Gallagher.'

'Oh.' She felt a strange mixture of feelings. 'Hello. What can I do for you?'

'I wondered if you'd heard anything of Tiffany. I've been trying to find her but she isn't at——'

'For heaven's sake!' Francesca yelled down the phone. 'Tiffany! Tiffany! I'm sick to death of hearing that name. I hope you never find her, because I've had enough of her to last me a lifetime!' And she slammed down the phone.

CHAPTER FOUR

'SHE wasn't there,' Chris said shortly as he came out on to the terrace and sat down beside her the next morning.

Francesca didn't bother to ask who. Looking up from the paper she was reading, she said, 'If anyone mentions that girl's name again, I shall scream. Do you want plain orange juice or Bucks Fizz?'

'Orange juice. I had enough champagne last night; I can't face it for breakfast as well.'

'Was it a good evening?'

'Yes, I suppose so.'

Francesca poured out the orange juice and glanced at her cousin. He was frowning, an abstracted look in his grey eyes. She sighed. 'All right, tell me if you want to.'

His lips twitched at her tone, but he shrugged and said, 'There's nothing to tell. I spoke to the landlord of the *pensão* but he was very surly, wouldn't tell me anything until I bribed him. Then he just said that Tiffany had been staying there but she hadn't paid any rent so he'd kicked her out.' His face grew grim. 'He said he didn't know where she'd gone and didn't care.' Chris's fingers tightened on his glass. 'I could have hit him. How could he have just turned her out into the street? He must have known she didn't have any money or anywhere to go.'

'Well, she's obviously found somewhere,' Francesca said shortly, fighting her own conscience. 'She was bound to; she's that type.'

Chris's eyes came up to her face. 'What's that supposed to mean?'

'It means that she must have found someone to look after her. She arouses that sort of instinct in men, with her little-girl-lost act. You, Sam Gallagher, you're both falling over yourselves to try and find her.' She didn't try to hide the resentment in her tone.

Chris gave a rueful smile. 'She does have that effect, I must admit. How do you know Sam is looking for her?'

'He rang me last night.'

'Did you tell him?' Chris demanded, his voice tense.

'No.'

It was only one word but she said it so curtly that Chris looked at her sharply. 'Sam's quite a character,' he remarked after a moment.

'Is he? I hadn't noticed.' Francesca glanced at her watch and pushed back her chair. 'I'd better change. I promised to go with Elaine to the hotel where we're holding the ball tomorrow, to make sure everything is running smoothly.'

'I gather you don't like Sam.'

'How could anyone possibly like someone so rude and uncivilised?'

'He didn't strike me that way.'

She gave a short laugh. '*You* didn't have to listen to his insults! He let Tiffany make a fool of him, but then blamed me for trying to put things right. He is the most ill-mannered, insolent man I have ever met,' she said with certainty. 'And just what are you grinning at?'

'I thought you said you hadn't noticed him.'

Francesca gave him a furious look and strode into the house.

Tonight the family were giving a dinner at the *palácio* for their fellow wine-growers, quite a small party when compared with the other celebrations that week. During the meal, Chris was called to the phone, then came back and said that he had to go out. Dinner was over before he returned, but most of the guests were still there so Francesca had no chance to speak to him privately. But she noticed something different about him, a sort of inner excitement. Looking at him, she suddenly knew: he had found Tiffany. It must have been her who had called him. What else would have been important enough to make him leave in the middle of dinner?

Francesca stirred uneasily, worried on her cousin's behalf. She could see nothing but trouble coming from such a relationship. Her instinct was to warn Chris off, to tell him to keep clear of Tiffany, but she realised that it wouldn't do any good. He was obviously besotted with the girl, even though he had no illusions about her. Chris knew what Tiffany was but he still wanted her.

Anger swept through Francesca, but all mixed up with jealousy and envy; there had been many men who'd wanted her, but she doubted if she'd ever aroused that particular look in a man's eyes that she'd seen in Chris's that evening. And all for a no-good, lying little tramp like Tiffany!

Even though her emotions were so mixed, Francesca's main concern was for Chris. Later that night, lying awake in bed, it occurred to her that she might be able to save him from himself. Picking up the phone, she called Sam at his hotel.

It was a couple of minutes before he answered and his voice sounded sleepy. 'Yeah?'

'This is Francesca de Vieira.'

He groaned. 'Do you always make calls and visits in the middle of the night?'

'It's only two-thirty.'

'Is that early in Portugal?'

'Look, I have some information for you. Do you want to hear it or not?'

He sighed. 'Go ahead.'

'I think my cousin has found Tiffany Dean.'

There was a short silence. 'Which cousin?'

'Chris, of course.'

'What do you mean you *think* he's found her?'

'He was called away in the middle of dinner tonight and didn't come back for a couple of hours. I think she rang him.'

'So why are you telling me this?'

'You're interested in her, aren't you? You could find out where she is and persuade her to go with you instead.'

Sam gave a disbelieving laugh. 'Are you serious?'

'Of course I am,' Francesca answered impatiently. 'You could quite easily follow Chris when he goes to see her, then talk to her yourself. Offer her money, offer to take her back to America with you; I'm sure she'd jump at the chance.'

'You think so, do you?' Sam's voice sounded cold. 'And just why are you so keen to pass Tiffany on to me?'

'I should have thought that was obvious,' Francesca replied sweetly. 'You and she are quite clearly meant for each other.'

'I shall take that as the insult you intended,' Sam said shortly.

'Please do.' Becoming impatient, she said, 'Well? Are you going to act on it?'

'Maybe. What about Chris?'

'What about him?'

'He just might have something to say if I stepped in.'

'Oh, dear, I should have realised you'd be afraid of him,' Francesca said with mock-concern. Her voice changing, she added scornfully, 'But surely even you could think of some way of removing Tiffany from Oporto before Chris finds out that you're involved?'

There was a pause, and she could imagine Sam's face becoming as grim as his voice as he said, 'You know something, Princess? Someone, someday, is going to shake the living daylights out of you.'

'Like you, for instance?' she said scornfully.

'Me? Hell, no! But I sure would give a whole lot to be able to stand there and watch!' And Sam put down the receiver.

Francesca determined to watch Chris as carefully as possible the next day, hoping to see signs that Tiffany had decamped with Sam, but he went out early and she was kept busy all day with preparations for the ball that evening, which was to be the climax of the week's festivities. It was only in the evening, at the dance, that she saw Chris again, when he walked into the ballroom—with Tiffany on his arm!

Stunned, Francesca could only stare in amazement, but then Tiffany walked by with Chris and gave her such a triumphantly scornful smile that Francesca's heart filled with dismay. So Sam hadn't been successful. She ought to have known; Tiffany, a gold-digger to her fingertips, would have realised immediately that Chris was a far better financial bet than Sam. Powerfully attractive as he was, Sam wouldn't have been able to compete against Brodey money.

Francesca turned away to do her duty as a member of the family, to dance with those who asked her, to be

sociable to their guests. But she was aware of Tiffany
and Chris dancing, Tiffany apparently having a wonderful time as she smiled and laughed up at Chris.
Michel, still in Portugal despite Francesca's lack of
interest, strolled over to her. She had danced with him
earlier, out of politeness, but hadn't bothered to conceal
her boredom. He stood beside her for a moment,
watching the dancers on the floor, then nodded towards
Tiffany and said with a touch of malice, 'Our little gatecrasher is the belle of the ball. How beautiful she looks—
so petite, so perfect.'

'You should take her home and put her on a pedestal
in your château,' Francesca returned flippantly, taking
a drink from a passing waiter. 'I'm sure she's for sale
and will go to the highest bidder—but could you afford
her, I wonder?'

Anger flashed for a moment in Michel's eyes, but he
said, 'Oh, your cousin is welcome to her; she holds no
interest for me. Unlike the man she's with at the
moment.'

The band was between numbers and Francesca had
been standing with her back to the ballroom but now
she glanced over her bare shoulder and saw that Tiffany
was talking to Sam, and Chris nowhere in sight.
Francesca had known that he was here, that Calum had
invited him, but Sam had made no attempt to speak to
her. As she glanced across at them, Sam lifted his head
and their eyes met for a moment. She didn't nod or smile,
didn't even acknowledge him, merely turned away with
a bored look, but when the band started to play again
she noticed that Sam led Tiffany on to the floor to dance
with her.

A strangely intense anger filled Francesca. How dared
that little tramp come here and—and *flaunt* herself like

this? It was disgusting. Michel said something to her, but she didn't even hear. Chris had come into the ballroom and was looking round, for Tiffany presumably. Striding up to him, Francesca said furiously, 'Have you gone out of your mind? How *dare* you bring Tiffany here? Letting that presumptuous little gold-digger loose among all our friends and guests!' She waved an angry hand towards the dance-floor. 'Can't you see what she's like? Can't you see what she's trying to do? She——'

Francesca broke off as Chris suddenly took hold of her arm and pulled her on to the dance-floor, then held her tightly as he began to waltz her round the room towards the other couple, determination rather than rhythm in his stride. Guessing his purpose, and afraid that he might create a scene, Francesca tried to stop him, but Chris held her so firmly that they were up to the others within a couple of minutes. When they reached them, both Tiffany and Sam were laughing, apparently well-pleased with each other's company.

'Let's exchange partners, shall we?' Chris said, and pulled Tiffany away from Sam.

'Well, really!' Francesca said furiously, but Chris had already moved away. She went to walk off the floor, but Sam caught her hand.

'Chris said to *exchange* partners,' he pointed out.

'I don't want to dance with *you*,' Francesca said angrily. She put her hands against his chest to push him away, but it was like trying to move a wall, and for the second time she found herself dancing against her will.

'Exchanging partners isn't a Portuguese custom, then?'

'No, of course it isn't.'

'Well, that's good, because I sure as hell wouldn't have chosen to dance with you. But if you're so crazy to dance with me that you got Chris to do that, then I'm willing to oblige.'

Francesca's jaw dropped. 'Of course I didn't get him to do it,' she said angrily. 'I've already told you I don't want to——' She saw a gleam of amusement in Sam's eyes and broke off, realising he was playing with her. 'Did you go and see Tiffany?' she asked him.

'No.'

'Why not?'

'If Chris is taking care of her, she doesn't need my help.'

She gave a slight frown. 'You give up very easily. I thought you said you were keen on her?'

'No, that's what you said. I didn't.'

She blinked in surprise. 'But why else would you want to find her?'

'Because I thought she needed some help.'

Francesca looked up at him, wondering if he was just trying to save face, having lost Tiffany to Chris, or whether he was teasing her again. It was true that there was a quizzical expression in the dark eyes that looked back at her, but it was more as if Sam was prepared to be amused by whatever she might say next. Francesca stiffened a little and said sardonically, 'It was for purely altruistic motives, then, was it?'

'Oh, definitely,' Sam agreed.

'And are you in the habit of taking stray women under your wing?'

'Don't seem to get many stray women where I come from. It's mostly cattle and sheep that go straying.'

'Oh, for heaven's sake!' Francesca said exasperatedly. 'Do you want Tiffany or don't you?'

'That's none of your business, Princess.' His arm tightened around her waist as she went to pull indignantly away. 'But I talked to her just now and she didn't ask me to help her, so presumably she's happy for Chris to do it.'

'But I don't want Chris to get involved with her. You should have taken her away.'

Sam laughed. 'You know something, Francesca? Your mother hasn't brought you up right. Didn't she teach you that you have to be nice to a guy to get him to do what you want? You know, use your wiles, make him feel good, before you throw him to the lions.'

She smiled a little. 'Is that what the girls do in Wyoming?'

'Oh, sure.'

She gave him a contemplative look, wondering for the second time whether he had a girlfriend back home, or even a wife. She didn't ask, of course, but Sam raised an eyebrow and said, 'What are you thinking?'

'That the girls I know don't have to resort to such old-fashioned methods to get what they want,' she answered promptly. 'They see it and they go for it.'

'Is that what you do?'

Her hand moved restlessly in his and she turned her head away, not liking the turn the conversation had taken. The music stopped, luckily, and he let her go. Francesca turned to walk off the floor, then suddenly stood still so that Sam bumped into her. He started to apologise, then followed her gaze. Chris, his hand firmly under her elbow, was leading Tiffany out of the ballroom, and there was such tension in his face that neither Francesca nor Sam had any doubt as to where they were heading.

Francesca turned abruptly and walked out of a side-door, down the corridor and out into the hotel garden. Sam hesitated a moment then followed her.

Almost running, Francesca kept going until she came to a low wall surrounding the garden. It was topped by an ornate railing, which she reached out and clung to, gripping it hard. In the distance there was the sound of traffic and, further off, the steady pounding of the Atlantic Ocean on the shore.

'Francesca? Are you all right?'

She swung round on him angrily. 'Of course. I'm not so pathetic that I need help from some man.'

'Oh, sure. You're really tough,' Sam said derisively. 'As hard as nails. So why cut and run like that?'

'Because I can't bear to watch Chris making such a fool of himself, that's why,' she retorted angrily. 'Tiffany will bring him nothing but trouble. I know it. I just know it.'

'Chris knows what he's doing.'

'No, he doesn't. He's bewitched by her and he isn't thinking straight. Tiffany will hurt him, I'm sure of it.'

Sam came nearer to her so that he could see her face in the moonlight. 'You're very fond of your cousins, aren't you?'

'Yes, I am.' She hesitated, but then said, 'In some ways I'm closer to them than to anyone.'

But Sam didn't understand, and said, 'Are you jealous of Chris going with Tiffany?'

'Jealous! No, of course not.'

She said the words vehemently but they were only partly true. It was the look in Chris's eyes, in his face, that had so devastated her. There had been such outright need, such intense longing. She had never seen him look that way before, had seldom seen any man look that way, if it came to that. The phrase head over heels in love came into her mind. But could Chris possibly be in love with a girl like Tiffany? Surely it could only be concupiscence, and he would soon grow out of it once he'd taken her a few times? Francesca tried not to think of them together, but found that, deep down, she almost envied Tiffany the night she was to spend in her lover's arms.

It was still early in the year and a cool breeze blew from the sea. Francesca shivered and put up her hands to rub her bare arms. Taking off his jacket, Sam put it round her but kept his hands on the lapels as he said, 'So why did you rush away like that?'

'I told you why.' Her spirits recovering a little, she added, 'Anyway, just what has it got to do with you?'

Sam looked down at her, his expression unreadable, but then he gave a slight shrug and said, 'Perhaps nothing. Perhaps—this.' And, pulling her forward, he bent his head and kissed her.

Francesca's mouth fell open in surprise and he took full advantage of it. His lips were firm and yet soft at the same time, hard and yet yielding, demanding but giving, too. Francesca had been kissed many times, by many men, but seldom had she been taken completely by surprise like this, and seldom had a kiss been so—insidious. Her first reaction was to get angry and push Sam away, but there was something about his kiss that got to her. Maybe it was because she was feeling low; maybe it was because it was comforting to be wanted. *If* Sam wanted her; she wasn't at all sure that he did. He certainly hadn't shown any signs of it, and usually she was good at reading signs. But this kiss was so unexpected that she'd had no time to think.

When she didn't resist, his arms went round her, drew her closer. She knew that this was all wrong, that Sam was probably amusing himself, but his lips felt so warm, stealing up on her senses like incense, holding her quiescent in his embrace. To Francesca it seemed that the sea was closer, that the waves sounded much louder, but when he raised his head at last she knew that it was the pounding of her own heart.

'Well,' Sam said softly. 'I got less than I expected— and yet much, much more.'

'What did you expect to get?' Francesca asked, her voice sounding odd as she still listened to that unexpected beat within her.

'My head knocked off,' he admitted.

'And instead?'

Sam hesitated for a moment, a moment too long. Suddenly angry, Francesca swung away and tossed his jacket back at him. 'Now I suppose you'll go back home and boast to the other cowboys how you kissed a princess!' she gibed.

'That wasn't why. I——'

'Oh, really? Why, then? Because you were frustrated at losing Tiffany to Chris? Or just because you found it amusing to see what would happen?'

'No! Will you listen a minute?'

But she laughed, the sound just a little too high-pitched. 'Aren't you interested in why I let you? Why I didn't knock your head off?'

Sam had been about to reach out for her, his mouth open in protest, but he became still, his face suddenly wary. 'OK, so why?'

'Because *I* thought it might be amusing.'

Sam's face tightened. 'And was it?'

'Oh, very. Tell me, how do you think of yourself back home in Wyoming? As the local macho-man, as some kind of stud? Or are you married and just want a fling with the sexy European girls you've read about? Something to brag about to the boys when you get home?' She tossed her head. 'Well, *you're* certainly nothing to brag about. You should catch the first plane home, Sam, because you're out of your league here. Even Michel makes it more interesting than you, and he's boring enough, God knows.'

'Have you finished?' he said tightly.

Francesca laughed again. 'Oh, dear, have I offended you? Forget it. I shall. It was just an amusing experiment on both sides.' She turned away. 'I'm cold; I'm going in.'

But Sam reached out and pulled her back. 'Are you this rude to all men or is it just Americans that you have something against?' he demanded curtly.

She shrugged in apparent amusement. 'American men are no different from any others, I suppose.'

'And you don't have a good word for any of them, do you? What turned you into a man-hater, Francesca?'

'A man-hater?' She gave a brittle little laugh. 'Is that what you think? Well, maybe I am. There's certainly nothing about men that I don't know.'

Sam stared at her for a moment, then said, 'Just what did that husband of yours do to you to make you so vindictive?'

Her eyes flashed with anger. 'Mind your own business. That has nothing to do with you!'

'Oh, but I think it does. To me and every man whose path crosses yours.'

She looked at him for a moment, her face and the bare skin of her shoulders pale in the moonlight. The breeze died away, and the scent she used, subtle and delicate as an orchid, seemed to fill the air around them. He couldn't see the colour of her eyes, could only see that the lashes trembled, giving her a vulnerable, lost look. But her chin, above the long, graceful column of her neck, rose bravely as she said huskily, 'Go home, Sam. Go home before——' She broke off, then quickly turned and began to walk back through the garden.

'Francesca.'

Halfway across, she stopped as he called her name and looked back at him.

'Will you have lunch with me tomorrow?'

'No.' She went on again, reached the door, hesitated. 'All the family are having lunch together tomorrow.'

Sam's shoulders straightened. 'The day after?'

She shrugged. 'Perhaps.'

'Yes or no, Francesca.'

Immediately her temper flared. 'No, then.' And she went inside.

He caught her up in the corridor and moved in front of her, his wide shoulders blocking the way. 'Where and when?'

'Why should I want to have lunch with you?' she demanded, feigned boredom in her voice.

'Maybe the same reason that made me want to kiss you back there.'

Tilting her head, surveying him, Francesca remembered that beat of her heart, a sensation that she'd thought dead inside her. 'The *churrasqueira* in the Rua de Almada at one o'clock, the day after tomorrow,' she said shortly, then strode past him into the ballroom.

Sam must have left the ball almost at once, because Francesca didn't see him again that night. She went on dancing with their guests and looked her cool, sophisticated self, but somehow the pleasure had gone out of the evening, and she was glad when it finally ended in the early hours of the morning. It was Chris's fault; he shouldn't have gone off with that little tramp.

Calum, too, was angry about it. Driving back to the *palácio* in his car, he said, 'Chris had no right to bring Tiffany tonight.'

'I don't suppose he had much choice,' Francesca answered. 'He wanted her so badly that I think he would have agreed to anything to get her.'

Calum glanced at her. 'Perhaps you're right. But she's no good for him. Let's just hope he soon sees through her.'

'Or grows tired of her.'

'That too. The sooner that girl is out of our lives the better,' Calum said forcefully.

Lunch the next day was a late one, but Chris arrived only just in time. He kissed his mother but apart from that merely gave them a general greeting before taking his place at the table. Francesca tried to attract his eye, but he seemed engrossed in his own thoughts and didn't look in her direction.

The meal went on for a long time, all the family aware that this might be the last time that they were all together like this. Grandfather had stood up wonderfully well to all the festivities, but he looked very tired now, as if he had suddenly lost his strength now that he was no longer on show, reminding them all that he was still far from well. This time it was Calum who made the speech, the last one of that long, busy week. It was short, merely thanking Grandfather for the heritage he had given them all, but it made their hearts swell, and Grandfather had to cough to hide the lump in his throat.

After lunch the party began to break up, a whole procession of cars heading down the driveway: Stella and Lennox back to Madeira, Chris's parents to Lisbon, her own parents to their home near Paris. Michel had already gone; Francesca had said goodbye to him at the ball last night, without regret, glad that he had given up at last. Calum went to the wine-lodge for a couple of hours, and Grandfather up to his room to rest. Chris helped to see them off, then headed for his car to go back to Oporto, but Francesca ran to stop him.

'Wait, I want to talk to you.'

Chris's face tightened. 'I expect I can guess what about. But I don't want to discuss it,' he said shortly.

'Chris, I don't want to quarrel with you. And I'm not narrow-minded. You wanted Tiffany, she became— available, and so you took up her offer.' She gave a small shrug, but then raised troubled eyes to his. 'But why did you take her to the ball last night? It was so defiant, so unnecessary—and so unlike you.'

Chris paused, his hand on the door of his car. He gave a small sigh. 'It was what she wanted.'

'You mean—part of the deal? A condition?'

He nodded. 'Tiffany promised she wouldn't make a scene, and she kept her word.'

'Her just being there was disruptive enough,' Francesca said a little bitterly. 'Why else should she want to go?'

'I think it had to do with pride,' Chris said slowly. 'She didn't like the way you showed her up.'

'She shouldn't have lied, then,' Francesca said angrily, then, pleadingly, 'She's no good for you, Chris. Please be careful. She'll hurt us if she can.'

His mouth twisted grimly, but then he gave her a curious look and said, 'But you haven't asked me to give her up.'

'No.' She put her hands on either side of his face and looked up at him earnestly. 'I know you can't. Not yet. You want her too badly. But please Chris, dear, dear Chris, try not to become too obsessed. Be very careful—for all our sakes.'

His grey eyes, so like her own, looked at her for a moment, then he kissed her lightly. 'I'd better go. Calum wants to see me in his office.' His face became grim. 'I can guess what about.'

'Don't quarrel with him, Chris. We're family. Surely that means more to you than——' She broke off, biting her lip, aware that at the moment probably nothing mattered to Chris as much as being with Tiffany, taking her to bed and making love to her.

She stepped back, her cheeks a little red, embarrassment in her eyes. Chris didn't say anything, just got into the car and drove back to Oporto.

Francesca watched him go, then turned back to the *palácio*, realising that she had it more or less to herself. Wandering out into the garden, she sat on one of the seats overlooking the view across the hills. She was wondering what to do with her life, whether to stay here or go to one of her apartments, either in Rome or Paris. Somehow, neither of the latter appealed to her. She had been brought up to a cosmopolitan lifestyle and usually enjoyed the frenetic pace, but right now she couldn't think of one earthly reason why she should want to go to a busy city when she could relax here in this wonderful garden. And it would be nice to have Grandfather and Calum to herself for a while.

She wondered, too, whether to keep her date with Sam tomorrow. He had sent a corsage of pale yellow rosebuds to her mother that morning, thanking her, as his official hostess, for the hospitality he had received from the family. It was a nice touch, and one that Francesca hadn't expected from him. Her mother had worn the flowers when she'd driven away, their softness beautiful against the dark velvet of her suit.

Pulling her legs up on the seat, Francesca clasped her knees. How much longer was Sam likely to be in Oporto? Surely his holiday must come to an end soon? And then he would go back to Wyoming, to the ranch-house where he worked. Fleetingly she wondered about his life there. It seemed strange that he had come here, of all places. Strange that they had met at all, when they were so obviously from different circles, different lifestyles. Really, she knew very little about him. Maybe he, like Tiffany, was a con artist, out for what he could get.

And was he out to get her? Francesca thought about it, and decided it just wasn't worth the risk. Sam could sit in the restaurant and wait, because she definitely wasn't going to keep that stupid date which she should never have made.

But somehow Francesca found herself driving into town the next day and making her way to the traditional Portuguese restaurant where she had arranged to meet Sam. She was there merely out of politeness, she told herself firmly; once she had made the date it would have been bad manners not to keep it, even though she knew that she was probably going to be bored out of her mind. She blamed herself; she and Sam had absolutely nothing in common and it had been a mistake to make the date in the first place. It had been a stupid impulse which she now regretted.

It occurred to her that Sam might not be there himself; she had described the place very briefly, not even naming the restaurant, and he hadn't asked her to repeat it. If he was there it would prove . . . what? Fanciful thoughts came into her mind, but she pushed them out. The only thing it would prove was that Sam was halfway intelligent, that was all. Francesca walked up the Rua de Almada half hoping he wouldn't be there, convincing herself that it would be a relief and she'd be glad not to have to go through with it. But when she entered the restaurant, a fashionable place among the townspeople and a place where she was well-known, and mentioned Sam's name, the proprietor smiled and told her that Sam was waiting for her.

There were several people Francesca knew in the restaurant; she acknowledged them as she followed the waiter, then turned to greet Sam as the waiter stood aside. But then she stared in stunned surprise as she saw that Tiffany was also sitting at the table!

A riot of thoughts went through Francesca's head, all of them distasteful. How dared Sam do this to her? He stood up, made some remark about meeting Tiffany by accident. Not believing him for a second, Francesca lowered her voice and said, her tone full of anger, 'If this is your idea of a joke, then you have an extremely warped sense of humour.'

She went to leave, but Sam was standing close beside her and took hold of her arm. To her furious indignation, he used his strength to push her into the seat the waiter had pulled out for her, saying, 'Sit down, Princess. Join the party.'

He held her there for a few moments, and she could feel the power in his hand, knew that he wouldn't let her up without a struggle, without her making a scene

that would draw unwelcome attention to them. Her
eyes, bright with fury and resentment, met his, then
looked away.

Letting her go, Sam sat down and said, 'What would
you like to drink? Campari?'

She didn't answer, didn't even register that he'd taken
the trouble to remember her favourite drink, just waited
until he'd given the order to the waiter, then said furiously, 'How dare you plan this?'

Leaning back in his chair, Sam said easily, as if they
were carrying on a normal conversation, 'I didn't plan
it. As I said, Tiffany and I ran into each other quite by
accident.'

Turning away from the other girl, completely ignoring
her, Francesca said vehemently, 'Well, if you didn't plan
it, then *she* certainly did. I doubt very much if she ever
does anything "by accident".'

Tiffany leant forward, tried to intervene, but Francesca
swept on, 'If you think I'm going to sit here with that—
that——' she had been about to say 'tramp' but saw the
warning look that came into Sam's eyes and hastily
changed it '—with *her*, then you're crazy!'

'And just why shouldn't you sit with Tiffany?'

The warning in his voice had changed to menace, but
Francesca was so angry that he'd deliberately put her in
this situation, and full, too, deep down, of a feeling of
overwhelming disappointment, that she ignored it to say,
'I should have thought that was obvious.'

'So she crashed your party. And you showed her up
in front of your cousins. So that's it, quits.' Sam's jaw
thrust forward. 'And I'll damn well ask who I want to
lunch.'

'Not with me, you won't!' She became aware that the
people on the next table had heard her and were looking

towards them curiously. Lowering her voice to a fierce undertone, she said, 'Don't you know what she is? Do you really not know?'

Again Tiffany tried to interrupt, giving Sam one of her helpless, innocent looks, but Francesca was determined not to let her speak, so went on quickly, 'She's no better than a prostitute. Don't you understand? She *sold* herself to Chris. Where else do you think she got the clothes she's wearing? How else would she have been able to go to our ball?'

Sam was leaning forward to speak, his body tense, but Tiffany said shortly, 'Before you ask, it's quite true.'

Her admission surprised Francesca, but before she could think about it Sam said forcefully, 'I wasn't going to ask. And what the hell does it matter anyway?'

Francesca glared at him, realising that he was completely on Tiffany's side. She went to get to her feet and leave, but again Sam caught hold of her and held her still.

'No, stay where you are. And *you* listen,' he said with cold, implacable anger. 'Who the hell are you to judge Tiffany? Have you bothered to find out what drove her to do it? Any of it? Can't you see that she's the kind of girl who would have to be desperate to do something like that?' Francesca couldn't, and went to say so, but Sam's grip tightened on her wrist as he went on, 'And so what if she has known other men? At least she doesn't go through the hypocrisy of marriage and divorce. And what if Chris has given her clothes and money? Didn't your Italian prince give you clothes and money when you sold yourself to him for the title?'

Francesca flinched as if she'd been physically attacked. She stared at Sam, unable to believe that he had been so rude to her. And all in defence of that little slut!

A great wave of rage filled her, an anger deeper than she'd ever known and which held her frozen in her seat. The waiter walked up with Francesca's drink on a tray. 'Your drink, *senhora*.'

His innocent approach broke the tension that held her. '*Obrigado*,' she said, then picked up the drink and threw it in Sam's face.

Letting go of her wrist, he jerked back, but she was pleased to see that quite a lot of the liquid went over his jacket. His eyes filling with threatening anger, he said in a voice that swore retribution, 'You'll pay for that one day, *Princess*.'

Not in the least intimidated, Francesca rose from her seat and gave them both a look of flaming contempt. 'I'll leave you two together. You obviously deserve each other!' And she walked away, head high, ignoring the startled stares of the other diners.

Hurrying to the car park, Francesca drove over the bridge to the Brodey wine-lodge where Calum had his office, knowing that Chris would be there today. Still fuming with anger, she swept through the outer office, ignoring the people working there, and pushed open Calum's door. Both her cousins were there, standing before some charts on the wall, computer printouts in their hands. They swung round, startled looks on their faces, as she strode in.

'What is it?' Calum said quickly, seeing the tension in her face.

'This concerns Chris.'

For a moment neither man spoke, each realising the implications. Then Calum dropped the papers he was holding and walked out of the office, closing the door behind him.

'Well?'

Her voice venomous, Francesca said, 'It seems Tiffany is hedging her bets.'

'What do you mean?'

'She's in Oporto now—with Sam Gallagher.'

Chris's face tensed, became taut with scarcely suppressed anger. 'Where?'

She told him, and watched as Chris slammed out of the room. Good, she thought triumphantly. Now Sam would get more than just a glass of wine thrown at his face!

CHAPTER FIVE

WHEN Chris had gone, Calum came back into the office. 'What was all that about—or need I ask?'

Francesca, still fuming, said tersely, 'It was that man, that despicable man!'

Calum's eyebrows rose. 'Chris?'

'No, of course not Chris. I mean Sam Gallagher.'

'What has he done?'

'He insulted me. I threw my drink over him.'

'Did you, now?' Calum gave her an arrested look. 'And just where did this happen?'

'At a restaurant.'

'With the whole of Oporto looking on, I suppose,' he said wryly. 'Will you never learn, Francesca? Haven't you had enough publicity? You know it upsets Grandfather to read about you in the gossip columns.'

She felt a pang of guilt, but said, 'It was Sam's fault. No one has ever dared to speak to me like that.'

'What did he do—make a pass?'

She blinked. 'No, he said... It doesn't matter what he said. But it was extremely insulting. You ought to do something about it.'

'What?'

'Knock him down or something.'

A startled look came into Calum's eyes. 'Is that what Chris has gone to do?'

'I certainly hope so.'

He stared. 'I shouldn't have thought... Just what *did* Sam say to you to make Chris go off like that?'

Francesca looked at him, then dropped moodily into a chair. 'He hasn't gone because of that. I don't suppose he cares that I've been insulted any more than you do,' she said petulantly.

'Why, then?'

'I told him Sam was with Tiffany.'

'Did you, now? And is he?'

'Yes. He had the—the nerve to invite her to have lunch with us.'

Again Calum looked surprised. 'You were having lunch with Sam? I thought you didn't like him?'

'I don't. I only agreed because I felt sorry for him,' Francesca said, convincing herself. 'And then he *dared* to invite that lying little gold-digger along too.'

'Is that why you threw your drink at him?' Calum asked, trying to hide a glint of amusement.

'No.' Francesca sighed. 'Lord, I could do with a drink now. Have you got one?'

Calum's mouth widened into a grin. 'My dear girl, this *is* a wine cellar.'

She looked up, caught the amusement in his eyes, and they both laughed. Lifting a hand to push her hair back, Francesca said, 'We've got to do something about Chris. We can't just sit back and let that girl ruin his life.'

'We've warned him; there's nothing more we can do. Chris is old enough to control his own life.'

'But he isn't in control of it, not where Tiffany is concerned; that's just the trouble. He seems to be bewitched by her.' She frowned, then looked at her cousin contemplatively. 'Have you ever felt like that about anyone— as if nothing else in the world matters?'

Calum came to lean against the edge of his desk and, reaching down, took her hand. 'Once. I thought I was head over heels in love. I couldn't eat, couldn't sleep; I *ached* to have her.'

'And did you get the girl?' Francesca asked curiously.

'Oh, yes.'

'So why didn't you marry her?'

His face became expressionless and he gave a small shrug. 'Because I found out that it was only infatuation after all. Once the physical need was gone, there just wasn't anything—emotional—left.'

'How sad for you. You never told me that before.'

'No, well...' He straightened up. 'You'd better go and let me get on with some work.' Francesca got up obediently and made for the door. When she reached it, he said, 'Don't forget we're having dinner with Elaine Beresford this evening to say thank you for all her hard work during the past week.'

'No, I won't forget.' She hesitated. 'Calum, this experience you had; it hasn't put you off marriage, has it?'

'No, of course not. I fully intend to marry some day.' He gave a small grimace. 'But I'm not sure that I'd ever trust falling in love again.'

Francesca was of much the same opinion as she made her way back to the *palácio*. She too had fancied herself really in love once, when she was at college in America. Andy had been a fellow student, brilliant at sports, a college hero. Francesca had fallen for him and he had said he felt the same. She could still remember those months when she'd felt herself in heaven, had known that life could never be better. Their backgrounds had been very different, Andy coming from quite a poor family and at college on a sports scholarship. But at college it hadn't mattered—he'd been the prize, she his devoted hero-worshipper, glorying in reflected popularity. Her love for him had blinded Francesca to his faults, to the differences that their environments had engendered. She too had been besotted then, had even introduced him to her grandfather when he'd come to America to visit her.

But it had been not long after that visit that Andy had quit college and just disappeared from her life. He hadn't said goodbye, had never written, which had been a terrible blow to her young, trusting heart. She'd shown a proud face to the world, but inside she had been badly hurt. Trust had died, and she had grown a shell around her heart.

The only person she had ever discussed Andy with was her grandfather. She had gone to him for comfort and he had gently pointed out all the differences between the two of them, had tried to make her realise that maybe it was better that Andy had gone, although he didn't expect her to see that for a while. He had been right, although it was taking a lot longer than he could possibly have envisaged; Francesca's heart had still not recovered from the results of that bitter blow. She too had quit college, and plunged headlong into the jet-set life that had led her inexorably to that hell of a marriage with Paolo de Vieira.

Her face tightening, Francesca determinedly pushed all thoughts of the latter out of her mind, just as she had deliberately tried to forget Andy all those years ago; she'd been so successful that now it was difficult even to remember his name. Only the hurt he had caused remained constant.

The weather turned cool and it began to rain, so she couldn't seek solace in the garden or the pool. Instead she played chess with her grandfather until she heard Chris come home, then she excused herself and ran up to his room. He had thrown his jacket on the bed and was pulling off his tie.

'What happened?' Francesca demanded, searching his face, looking for signs of a fight and finding none.

'Sam said they ran into each other in the town,' Chris said tersely. 'He said she left soon after you did.'

'I don't believe that.'

Chris suddenly rounded on her angrily. 'I don't much care what you believe, Francesca. Just keep out of this.'

'Did Sam say anything else?'

'We exchanged a few words,' he admitted, unbuttoning his shirt.

'Did you hit him?' she asked rather breathlessly.

'No, Francesca, I didn't hit him.'

'You should have done; he was extremely rude to me.'

'Why—because you told him that I was taking care of Tiffany?'

She gave a sound very like a sniff. 'I'd hardly call it that.'

Chris swung round and caught her by the arms, his shirt flying open. 'I don't give a damn what you call it, or what you think of it. My arrangement with Tiffany is my business and you had no right to tell Sam or anyone else about it. Do you understand?'

'But she's no good for you,' Francesca protested fiercely. 'She'll only make trouble for you and——'

Her words were broken off as Chris gave her an angry shake. 'Shut up, Francesca. Just shut up! I'm sick of you and Calum telling me to stay away from Tiffany. It's between her and me, no one else.'

Putting her hands on his chest, she started to say pleadingly, 'Please, Chris, think about this before you go too far. You know nothing about Tiffany. For all you know she——'

But Chris pushed her angrily away and propelled her towards the door. 'Get out, Francesca. Get out and mind your own business. I'm leaving here and I'm taking Tiffany with me.'

'What? But you can't poss——' Francesca stopped abruptly as he pushed her out of the room and shut the door in her face. Slowly she turned and went to her own room, deeply worried for her cousin. Chris was an attractive man, not only physically but financially too. Tiffany would be out to hook him, to use his infatuation for her to get Chris to marry her. Then she would make him bring her back here so that she could flaunt herself in front of the family, to taunt them with her victory. Francesca could imagine Tiffany's vindictiveness, her spite. She would get as much out of Chris as she possibly could, hurt and embarrass them all as much as she could. But that didn't matter; it was only the harm she would do to Chris that mattered.

As she showered and changed for dinner, Francesca's thoughts were filled with anxiety. How could Chris have possibly walked into such a relationship, especially when he knew Tiffany for what she was? It was crazy! Madness!

She said as much to Calum when she went down to the drawing-room for a pre-dinner drink. He agreed with her, but again said that Chris would very likely tire of Tiffany very quickly. They had to break off the conversation then because Elaine came to join them. Grandfather had gone to spend the evening with friends at the Factory House, so the three of them were going out to dinner in town.

Elaine, the responsibility of the last week over, looked very relaxed tonight and very elegant. While she was working she tended to wear businesslike clothes, but she obviously saw tonight as a holiday and had dressed accordingly, in an evening dress of subtle shades of green that enhanced the sea-green of her eyes. Usually, too, she wore her hair in a sensible French pleat, giving her face a rather severe look, but tonight she had let it fall into a thick mane of burnished copper, just clipped back from her face. Calum's eyes widened a little when he saw her and, although he had always been friendly and polite towards her, his manner seemed to change a little, as if he saw Elaine now as an attractive woman, not just the caterer.

Francesca noticed with inner surprise and wondered if she was going to play gooseberry tonight, but Calum was far too well-mannered to give Elaine all his attention. They finished their drinks and he went to bring his car round, as he was driving them himself this evening. Francesca and Elaine went into the hall to wait, chatting easily about mutual acquaintances and Elaine's future plans. She was staying at the *palácio* at the moment, but Calum had offered her the use of the house at the *quinta* for a holiday, and she hoped to be able to accept.

A car drew up outside. Francesca opened the door and they went out on to the steps. But it wasn't Calum's car. It was an ordinary small saloon which Francesca immediately recognised. She gave a small gasp but had no time to do anything before Sam climbed out and came towards them.

Recovering, Francesca glared at Sam and said icily, 'I should have thought that even someone as insensitive as you would have realised that you're no longer welcome in this house.'

Beside her, Elaine caught her breath in surprise, but Sam seemed quite unperturbed as he came on up the steps. 'I was hoping you'd be here, Princess.'

'Don't call me that,' she snapped at him. 'And please leave.'

Calum's car came round the side of the house and he pulled up alongside Sam's. Getting out, he looked at Sam watchfully. 'Good evening, Sam.'

Sam nodded in return. 'Calum.'

'Francesca tells me you—had a disagreement earlier today.'

'I guessed she might have told you—just like she went running to Chris and told him,' Sam said calmly, his eyes on Francesca.

She didn't like the glint in his eyes, wasn't at all happy about him being there. Taking hold of Elaine's arm, she said, 'We're just going out to dinner. Come along, Elaine.' And she pulled the other girl towards Calum's car.

But Sam stepped in the way and said, 'Good, you can have dinner with me instead—after all, you promised to have a meal with me today.'

'You're crazy,' Francesca gasped. 'After the way you spoke to me today, I wouldn't go anywhere with you.'

Sam heard, but he took no notice. Turning to Calum, he said pointedly, 'Don't let us keep you.'

Calum frowned. 'I don't know what you said to Francesca at lunchtime, but——'

'She didn't tell you? I'm amazed. I told her she married the Prince for his title and that she's no better than Tiffany.'

'Ahem.' Calum made a strange noise in his throat. 'Yes, I see,' he said faintly. 'And do you intend to insult her again now?'

'I guess it's pretty likely,' Sam admitted.

'I see,' Calum repeated.

Francesca, losing patience, said hotly, 'Don't just stand there saying "I see". Throw him out.'

'I'd like to help you,' Calum answered, 'but somehow I don't think he'd go.' And, putting a hand under Elaine's elbow, he helped her into the car.

Her mouth falling open in astonishment, Francesca said, 'You're—you're not going to leave me with this—this moron?'

'Well, I am rather hungry.'

With that, Calum, too, got in the car and, to her intense indignation, drove away.

'The coward!' she exclaimed furiously. Then she rounded on Sam. 'What do they call you back in Wyoming—Jumbo? Because you're certainly as thick-skinned as an elephant. You can just get back in your car and get out of——'

Taking a purposeful step towards her, Sam put his hands on either side of her face and silenced her mouth with his own. Again she had no warning of what he was going to do, but this time she recovered more quickly and clawed at his hands with her nails. Sam swore, swooped down and put his arms round her legs, then slung her over his shoulder.

Francesca gave a shriek of disbelief, then began to thump her clenched fists against his back and to struggle in his hold. She might just as well not have bothered: Sam didn't even seem to notice as he strode round the house and down into the garden. He carried her through the parterre, past the flowerbeds and shrubberies, on down the steps to the terrace overlooking the fruit-gardens and the hillside. Only then, when they were well away from the house, did he set her on her feet. Seething

with rage, her eyes shafting arrows of fire, Francesca
came up fighting—but Sam calmly pulled her into his
arms and kissed her again.

She would have fought him, but his arm was round
her and held her prisoner. She would have denied him
her mouth, but he put his free hand behind her head
and held her still while his lips seared hers. She would
have kicked out at him, but he was bending her back,
her body pressed against his, and she would have lost
her balance if she'd tried. She would have cursed and
sworn at him, but her senses began to reel under the
onslaught of his mouth. Anger, outrage, indignation—
all began to fade before the compulsive demands of his
lips. Her heart began to beat in that crazy way again,
and she felt an ache that was almost a stranger begin to
grow deep within her.

All she managed was a gasp that became a long, low
sigh of discovery.

Her mouth opened under his, accepted the exploring
softness of his tongue, then slowly yielded to the demand
of his kiss by giving him the response he wanted.

Sam straightened up, loosened his hold a little, so that
Francesca's arms were free. They crept up round his neck,
still a little reluctant, but as that ache within her took
hold her hands suddenly gripped his shoulders convul-
sively. From a tentative reaction, her mouth sponta-
neously became a living flame, returning his kiss so
ardently that Sam gasped with shock, before he too let
passion flare.

His hand tightened in her hair and his mouth left hers
to rain kisses on her throat. Francesca moaned but she
pulled him back, still greedy for his mouth. They were
both panting with heat, with excitement. Sam's hand
went down low on her waist to hold her against him, to

excite the growing hardness of his body. Francesca's
hands were in his hair, clutching his shoulders, and she
made little animal sounds deep in her throat as she went
on kissing him, so avidly, with such abandonment.

She was wearing a sequinned jacket over her dress, a
dress that had just shoestring straps which tied in bows
on her shoulders. Sam's hands went to her jacket, pulled
it off and let it fall. His mouth traced her jawline, her
throat, the seductive line of her bare shoulder. His teeth
found the end of the bow and pulled it loose. The straps,
the soft material, fell, revealing the swell of her breast,
her skin pale and silken in the moonlight. Sam lifted his
head a little to look at her. She felt his body jerk in
awareness, and pressed her hips against his, the ache now
an avid, overwhelmingly urgent need.

Sam groaned, a long, low sound of primitive hunger.
His lips caressed her shoulder-blade, burning her skin,
then went on down, a trail of fire. The softness of his
lips on her already aroused and sensitive nipple drove
Francesca into a frenzy. Her cry of pleasure, of tor-
mented awareness, echoed through the gardens, across
the hillside. She said his name, breathless, urgent, then,
unable to stand the exquisite torture of it, she dragged
his head up to take her lips again. He did so compulsively, until the world spun around their heads and their
breath was one long, gasping moan of passionate desire.

It was impossible to go on with such intensity. Sam
lifted his head, his breathing ragged, and held her against
his shoulder. Francesca felt as if she had two hearts—
her own pounding in her chest, and Sam's beating almost
as loudly under her ear. Her brain, her mind, wasn't
working; she was consumed by her own emotions, by

the physical, sexual sensations that Sam had aroused in her.

'Oh, Francesca.' His arms tightened around her as he said her name on an unsteady note of discovery.

Francesca closed her eyes, overwhelmed by this new and so unexpected happiness. For the moment she didn't question how such a thing could have happened; she was content just to know that it had, to be held close in Sam's arms and to feel the strength of him against her.

His lips brushed her hair and she lifted her face to smile at him tremulously. Raising her hand, she let it gently stroke his face, exploring the flat planes of his cheeks, the strong firmness of his jawline. Her finger followed the line of his straight brows, then traced the lips that had so aroused her. Catching her hand, he held the palm against his lips for a long, tense moment, then kissed her fingers one by one. 'I'm crazy about you, Francesca,' he said huskily. 'I fell for you the moment I saw you.'

'Really?' She smiled, her eyes tender. 'I would never have known.'

Sam grinned at her, gave her a fierce hug, like a bear, then, to her surprise, let her go and began to re-tie her bow. He found her jacket and held it for her to put on. His hand slipped to her waist, stayed there for a moment as he gazed at her, as if registering the way she looked— her features soft and still sensual—imprinting it on his mind forever. From there, his eyes turned to the moonlit hillside, to the distant silver snake of the river as it meandered towards the sea. A small sigh of contentment escaped him, then, taking her hand, he led her back through the gardens.

Francesca had no doubt that after the intense passion of that kiss Sam was taking her back to his hotel, to his bed. And she wanted that. Her body, her senses were still trembling with excitement and need. She couldn't remember ever having felt such overwhelming sexual desire as this. Long ago, when she'd been at college and fallen for Andy, perhaps? But no, even that first all-consuming awareness of womanhood hadn't been as strong as this. And she certainly hadn't felt anything like it during that degrading mistake of a marriage with Paolo. Now she was eager to go to bed with Sam, longed to feel again that consuming passion, and to have that passion returned and fulfilled.

Her high heels slowed her down on the grass, and Sam said, 'Would you rather we walked through the house than round it?'

'We can't get through; these doors at the back are locked and I don't have a key. And we can't ring for a maid to open them because all the servants have been given the night off.'

'You mean the house is empty?'

'Yes.'

Sam came to a stop. 'Do you have a key for the front door?'

She looked up at him, saw a blaze of excitement in his eyes, and caught her breath. 'Yes,' she nodded.

'Come on, then.'

They walked round to the front, Francesca gave Sam the key, he unlocked the door and they went into the lighted hallway. There he stopped, gave a big grin, and to her amazement said, 'Which way is the kitchen?'

'The *kitchen*?'

'Sure. I'm hungry. Aren't you?'

Francesca definitely was hungry, but it wasn't that kind of hunger. 'Do you really want to—eat?'

The way she said it, the invitation in her eyes, made Sam catch his breath. For a moment he stood very still, then he bent and gently touched his lips against hers, so soft, so sensual. He straightened and gave her one of his lazy smiles, but there was a warmth in it, a promise, that she had never seen before. 'Yeah, I'm hungry. Let's see what we can find and have a picnic.'

That impromptu meal was one Francesca would always remember. They raided the refrigerator and the wine cellar, carried their spoils up to the sitting-room and ate sitting on cushions on the floor. As Sam said, 'A picnic isn't a picnic if you sit at a table.'

They feasted on chicken and home-cured ham, crispy bread and *pâté de foie gras*. They ate fresh fruit from the garden and hothouses, biting into lush peaches and grapes. They drank claret and champagne, clinked their glasses and made silent toasts as they looked into each other's eyes. And their eyes said it all; spoke of awakened, recognised need and made the promise to fulfil it.

Francesca had put on some music, soft, instrumental tunes which formed a fitting background to this love feast. They didn't talk very much, were content to listen to the music, to look at each other, to smile and laugh over the smallest, silliest thing, such as when Sam opened the champagne and it frothed over. Francesca came quickly up on to her knees with a glass to catch it, but her closeness made Sam kiss her, both of them unaware of the champagne flowing over their hands.

Coming to sit beside her, their backs against a sofa, Sam with his legs stretched out in front of him, Francesca with hers curled to the side, Sam put his arm round her and held her comfortably against his shoulder. His eyes fell on a nearby table full of family portraits in their silver frames. He nodded towards them. 'Is that innocent-looking little cherub really you?'

She laughed. 'Yes, but it was taken a long time ago.'

'Tell me about when you were young. Tell me everything about yourself,' Sam commanded.

But she didn't want to talk, and definitely not about herself. So instead Francesca reached up to put her hand on his face and then kissed him. She felt a quiver of awareness go through him as her mouth explored his, softly, tantalisingly. She didn't let passion come into it, not yet; instead she played with his mouth, raining little kisses on his lips, letting her tongue just touch his and then draw away again. Her hand gently caressed his face, his throat, her fingertips running lightly, seductively over his skin. Sam's breathing changed, became faster, and only then did she get up on her knees, put both hands on his face, and let desire impassion her kiss.

Pulling her on to his lap, Sam bent his head over hers, returning her kiss with profound intensity. There was desire there and passion, but somehow the kiss went deeper than that; it carried her down a mystical, sunlit tunnel in which she could feel nothing but the wonder of his lips on hers and the clamour of her own desire.

When he lifted his head at last, Francesca gave a long sigh and said huskily, 'Take me to bed, Sam. I want you so much.'

He put an unsteady hand on her face, his breath a wondering, panting gasp. 'Francesca! My beautiful, beautiful girl. Do you mean it?'

'Oh, yes. Oh, yes.'

He held her to him, then said raggedly, 'I want you to come to America with me. I want you to see where I live before you make up your mind. I want you to be absolutely sure that you're not going to make another mistake.'

Not really listening, her body impatient now, Francesca said, 'I'm sure. Let's go up to my room.'

'Here? No.'

'Let's go back to your hotel, then.' She kissed him again, her mouth fervent, the ache inside her growing to a ravenous hunger.

But Sam took hold of her wrists and held her a little away from him so that she could see his face. 'Francesca, listen to me. I want to make love to you more than anything I've ever wanted in my life. But I want to do this right. I'm in love with you. I want you to marry me; to come back to America and spend the rest of your life with me. And it would be for keeps, my darling. If you give yourself to me, then you give yourself forever.'

Francesca's eyes slowly opened wide as she stared at him. 'You want to—marry me?'

'More than anything in the world,' he said in simple assurance.

'But...' She felt a *frisson* of fear and slid off his lap on to her knees as she stared at him. 'But I don't *know* you.'

'That's why I want you to come home with me, to see where——'

Her voice changing, becoming harsh, Francesca said curtly, 'You think because I let you kiss me, because I'm willing to go to bed with you, that I want to marry you? You must be crazy!'

Sam looked into her face and his features tightened. 'What are you saying, Francesca? That this is nothing but sex?'

'Of course it's nothing but sex. What else would it be? Do you really think I'm going to give up everything and live in some log cabin just because we fancy each other?'

'Stranger things have happened,' Sam said shortly.

'Not to me, they don't! I've had one disastrous marriage and I sure as hell don't intend to make the same mistake again.'

'I don't want you to make a mistake. That's why I asked you to come out there with me and see for yourself. I can take care of you, Francesca; you needn't be afraid of that.'

Taking a deep breath, Francesca said as calmly as she could, 'I think I already made a mistake. Look, Sam, I'm sorry if you got the wrong idea. I don't want to marry you. Can't you see that it would be impossible? We're so different.' She spread her hands helplessly. 'Surely you can see that?'

His voice grim, Sam said, 'You mean that you're so rich, so used to leading a jet-set lifestyle?'

'Yes, exactly that,' Francesca agreed, her chin rising.

'Yet you were willing to go to bed with me—and right then you didn't give a damn about our so-called differences. You *wanted* me. You wanted me to make love to you because you knew that we were right for each other.'

'In bed perhaps. But for keeps?' She shook her head emphatically. 'No way, Sam. I'm sorry.'

'You will be if you let the happiness I can give you go.'

'No.' She got to her feet. 'I know I'm right about this.'

Sam quickly stood up beside her. There was a dark glint in his eyes and his teeth were gritted together. For a moment Francesca expected him to take her in his arms again, to try to kiss her into submission, to dominate her with the physical need he had aroused in her before. It was the act she expected of such a strongly masculine man. She was ready to fight him, to show him how much she despised him for it—but Sam made no move towards her, instead looking at her with a strange, grim kind of smile.

'I feel sorry for you, Francesca. You've been so hurt in the past that you're afraid to let yourself fall in love, afraid to acknowledge your own feelings. We're right for each other. I know that. Maybe you will too one day.'

She shook her head, outwardly firm, but inwardly disturbed by his certainty. She saw that his hands were clenched, his features taut, and she realised how deeply he must be feeling this. An alien, fluttering sensation filled her heart, and for a moment she was strongly tempted to run to him, to kiss away the grimness in his eyes, to soften the line of his mouth. But she fought it down and said shortly, 'If you know that I've been hurt, then you ought to realise that there's no way I would commit myself to anyone else unless I was absolutely sure.'

'I'm not asking you to commit yourself. I'm asking you to come with me to see how I live and get to know me and my world better. To give us a chance.'

'But you asked me to marry you.'

'Because I want to be honest with you. I'm not going to take you to bed, have an affair, and just hope that you'll eventually agree to marriage. I could do that, and I think our lovemaking would be so good, so passionate, that I could persuade you to marry me, perhaps against your own will.' His eyes, dark with intensity, settled on her face. 'But I love you too much for that. I want you to be as eager and willing as I am. This is the most wonderful thing that has ever happened to me,' he said with sincerity. 'And I want it to be that way for you too.'

'Oh, Sam.' Francesca looked into his face for a long
moment, and thought how easy it would be to go along
with him, to say, Yes, take me with you, to let his love
be strong enough for them both. But she knew she
couldn't do it. She was too scared, too afraid to trust
another man, even to trust herself. Shaking her head
decisively, she said, 'It wouldn't work. I'd make both
our lives miserable.'

'You don't know that unless you give it a try.'

'But I do know.' Going to him, she put her hands
against his chest. His jacket was off and he was wearing
just a thin shirt. Beneath it she could feel the smooth
planes of his chest, the tautness of his skin, the rise of
the minute nipples. She imagined what it would be like
to be held against him and feel his skin, silky against
her own, and was immediately aroused. She thought of
him naked, knew that he would be beautiful, and felt
the ache deep within her. Strong mental pictures of what
it would be like to go to bed with him filled her mind
and made her want him with a thrilling urgency.

Softly she said, 'But it doesn't have to end like this.
We need each other. We could still be together while
you're here in Portugal. I'd come to your room and we
could make love there. We could——'

Without warning, Sam took hold of her wrists and
pushed her violently away. 'What's that supposed to be?'
he demanded harshly. 'Some sort of consolation prize?
Don't you listen, Francesca? I just got through telling
you I don't want some cheap affair.'

Startled, embarrassed, and physically rejected for the
first time in her life, Francesca, her voice rising to an
angry yell, retorted, 'Cheap? What the hell do you mean,
cheap? Do you think I go around offering myself to every
man that comes on strong?' Her chin came up. 'There

is *nothing* cheap about me. I haven't had a man since my marriage broke up. Not in over two years! You would have been the first. But now I'm glad that you said no, because I was out of my mind even to contemplate going to bed with you. I must have been mad, crazy!'

Sam took a step towards her. 'Listen to me, Francesca.'

'No! Who the hell do you think you are, walking into my life and trying to take it over? You're nothing, do you understand? Just a jumped-up cowboy from the backwoods.' Francesca's eyes hardened as she said jeeringly, 'Marry you? You must be joking! Give up everything just to go and live in some shack in the middle of nowhere for the rest of my life? Be content with that just because you happened to turn me on? Or were you contemplating living on my money? Was that it? Have you got a taste for the high life now and expect me to pay for it?'

'If you say one more word...' Sam began menacingly.

But, too angry to care, Francesca swept on, 'Do you really think I'd become the laughing-stock of everyone I know? Dragging you around Europe, watching you make a fool of yourself. You're out of your class, Sam. To us you're a nobody. So get out of here.' Her voice rose to an hysterical pitch. 'Just get out of here!'

Sam's hands had balled into fists again, but of fury this time. He took a menacing step towards her, and maybe he would have been enraged enough to put her over his knee and give her the spanking he'd once promised. Or maybe this time he would have taken hold of her and kissed her into admitting she was wrong. But which course he would have chosen Francesca never knew, because the door opened and Calum strode quickly into the room.

'What's going on?' he demanded. 'I heard you yelling out in the hall.' He looked round the room and saw the remains of their picnic, saw the taut anger in their faces. 'I think I came in at the wrong moment,' he said wryly.

'You sure did,' Sam said tersely.

'No, you came at the right moment. Sam is just leaving.'

'I take it you insulted her again, Sam?'

Sam gave a harsh, mirthless laugh. 'Oh, sure, the worst insult I could throw at her, it seems.'

Francesca flushed, fighting down a sudden feeling that she had behaved badly. 'Please, just go away, Sam.'

He didn't move straight away, just stood looking at her, his mouth twisted into a wry, bitter smile. Then he turned and strode away without a word.

When he'd gone, when they'd heard the front door slam, Calum came further into the room and said, 'Did he really insult you?'

Francesca sighed and put up a hand to push aside her hair. 'I suppose you could call it that; he asked me to marry him.'

His eyes widened. 'You took that as an *insult*?'

'I suppose I did.' She stirred restlessly. 'But he insulted me first.'

'How?'

'It doesn't matter how. I just never want to see him again.'

Studying her face, Calum saw the tension in it, the lost look in her eyes. 'Are you sure you're not making a very big mistake, Frankie?' he asked, using the diminutive of her name that she'd outgrown years ago.

Tears threatened her eyes. 'Of course I'm sure. It wouldn't have worked. He wanted to tie me down to some cabin on a cattle ranch. I couldn't have stood that. If he really loves me it——'

'Which I think he does,' her cousin interrupted.

'OK, maybe he does. But I could never lead the life he wants and I would have hurt him unbearably. It would have hurt us both. And I've had enough hurt in my life. I'm not going to take even the smallest chance of it happening again.'

Frowning, seeming to pick his words, Calum said, 'Did Sam actually say that was what he wanted—for you to live in a cabin on a ranch?'

'More or less. He said he wanted me to go to America with him, to find out more about him and his lifestyle.'

'That was all he said?'

'Except for saying he wanted to marry me.'

Calum's frown deepened and he hesitated before saying, 'How do you feel towards him?'

Unable to describe the chemistry that had erupted between them, unable to tell him that Sam had rejected her offer to go to bed with him, Francesca just shrugged and said, 'He's OK.'

'Just OK?'

'Yes.' She turned to look for her shoes, hiding her face. Picking them up, she said, 'I'm tired. I'm going to bed.'

'Francesca, I really think that you and Sam——'

She rounded on him. 'I don't want to talk about him. It's boring. I wish he'd go back to the States. I wish he'd never come here.' And she strode out of the door.

But Sam came again the next morning. Francesca was sitting at the desk in the sitting-room, writing letters, when he was shown in. He didn't smile; his mouth was set in a thin line and the grim look was back in his eyes.

Without preamble, he said, 'I'm leaving for the States tomorrow morning. I've come to ask you one last time to come with me.'

Francesca's heart was thumping like a sledge-hammer and she found it difficult to speak. Licking lips gone dry, she managed to make her voice firm. 'No.'

It was all she said. Sam merely nodded, then turned and walked out of her life.

Francesca stared after him, somehow not having expected him to accept her refusal like that. She'd expected him to plead, or to put on a masterful act. That he'd just walked out was strangely disconcerting. Blinking, she turned back to her desk, and told herself she was glad, she was relieved it was all over, that she'd been a fool to let it get out of hand in the first place. But she put a hand up to her eyes and smudged the make-up that had disguised a sleepless night.

CHAPTER SIX

FOR the next three weeks Francesca stayed at the *palácio*. During the first week she spent a couple of days with Elaine at the *quinta*, but then Calum came down to join them over the weekend, and to her surprise he intimated that she was in the way. So Francesca left them there together, giving their relationship a chance to—to what? Develop into an affair, she supposed. And she wondered if Calum had offered the use of the *quinta* to Elaine for just that reason. The dubious devil, she thought with a grin as she drove alone back to Oporto.

But back at the house, with just Grandfather for company, and that not very often because he always seemed to be going out somewhere now that he was so much better, Francesca began to feel distinctly lonely. The weather was warm so she was able to swim and sunbathe by the pool; she caught up on a few old friendships, although she didn't really know anyone in Oporto well because she'd spent most of her childhood in France. But there were some people whom she'd known from when she'd come here for holidays—the children of other wine-growers, mostly. Francesca found, though, that all the girls still living in the area were married, several of them with children. She paid each of them a visit, but found that you could only talk about old, shared experiences for a limited time, and she just wasn't into listening to endless stories about their offspring, no matter how delightful.

When Calum came back it was better, but he was annoyingly reticent about the days he'd spent at the *quinta*
with Elaine. If it had been Chris, Francesca might have
come right out and asked him if he and Elaine had gone
to bed together, but there was something about Calum
that stopped you asking him such a personal question,
even when you knew him as well as she did. And he gave
little away in his manner, although a couple of times she
did catch him gazing into space with a slight frown
creasing his forehead. But that could be work, or
anything.

If it came to that, she was doing quite a lot of gazing
into space herself. It was Sam Gallagher's fault, damn
him! Why did he have to make that absolutely stupid
proposal? It had stirred up feelings she wasn't at all
familiar with: guilt for one. Although why the hell *she*
should feel guilty Francesca didn't know. It wasn't her
fault that the fool of a man had fallen for her. It wasn't
even her fault that she'd fancied him; one couldn't
control something like that. As far as she was concerned
it was just her bad luck to have wanted a casual affair
with someone who'd gone serious on her. Especially
when she'd been without a man for so long...

When Francesca thought about Sam and the tem-
pestuous kisses they'd exchanged, the ache of longing
came back and seemed to burn within her. She felt
restless and unsettled, couldn't laze about as she'd intended, instead having to get up and walk around, look
for something to occupy her, someone to talk to. Driven
to distraction by it, she ended up thumping her fist
against the wall and thinking, God, I've got to have a
man!

Francesca fought this frustration in the way that many
women did: she went shopping. But the stores in Oporto

were as nothing compared to those in Paris and Rome. And somehow her heart just wasn't in it, especially when it began to rain solidly for days and seemed as if it was never going to stop. Standing at the window of the sitting-room looking out at the sheets of water that descended endlessly from the looming grey sky, Francesca was unable to stop her thoughts turning to that last night with Sam, when they'd had a picnic in this very room. She wondered what would have happened if Sam hadn't been such a fool, if he'd taken her to bed as they'd both wanted.

Closing her eyes, she could see it in her imagination; slowly undressing each other, and then their bodies entwined, naked on a large bed, his hands exploring, his lips lighting fires of urgent hunger as they trailed all over her. Her hand went to cover the breast he had kissed as she remembered again the heat of his mouth, the sensations of overwhelming desire. She felt the taste of his mouth against hers, his lips so demanding, so sensual. Then she pictured him taking her, his big body thrusting strongly into hers. She could almost hear the rasping of his breath, his groans of desire, feel the thudding of his heart and the hardness of his body against her hips, feeling the ache, the desperate longing...

Francesca swung away from the window, her breath gasping as if she'd run a long way. She clutched hold of the back of a chair, her legs suddenly weak and unsteady. She moved her hips, trying to quell the fire that burned there, and gave a long, low moan of desperate frustration and need. She stood there for a long time, then slumped into a chair, her emotions as wild and chaotic as her thoughts.

She was still there when Calum came home from the office, sitting in the semi-darkness, the dreary rain still pelting down outside, beating against the window-panes, splashing in the puddles on the terrace. He came in, flicking on the light, then stopped in surprise.

'Francesca! Are you all right?'

She lifted her head, blinking against the light. 'Oh! Yes, fine.'

'Why are you sitting in the dark?'

'Was I?' She looked towards the window, only now realising how late it was. She shivered and put her hands up to rub her arms. 'Lord, I hate this rain.'

Coming to sit beside her, he put his arm round her and said, 'What is it, Frankie?'

She managed a smile at that and leaned her head against his shoulder. 'Just the rain.'

Calum looked at her bent head for a moment, his brows drawn into a frown. 'You're not missing Sam by any chance?'

'Sam Gallagher?' She sat up, her face becoming bland. 'Of course not. Why on earth should I miss him?' she said offhandedly.

He shrugged. 'You seem very low, that's all.' He paused, but when Francesca didn't speak he said, 'Do you remember I said I'd look out for something for you to do? Well, how would you like to work for the company?'

Swinging round to face him, her eyes lighting up, she said, 'How do you mean? Work here in the office with you, or at the *quinta*?'

'No, I thought you might get bored doing that. But it occurred to me that as this is our bicentennial year we'll be holding celebration parties all over the world for our customers. I wondered if you'd like the job of organising and coordinating them. Well, what do you think?'

'Oh, Calum, I'd love it. Do you mean it?'

'Yes, of course.'

'I organised several parties when I was married, but I don't have a great deal of experience, you know,' she felt bound to say.

'You organised the celebrations here extremely well. But I don't expect you to actually order the food and drink. I thought that perhaps we might get Elaine's company to do that, at least for the parties in Madeira. But you would have to organise dates and guest-lists, liaise with our offices in the various countries and——' He broke off. 'Why are you sitting there with that huge grin on your face, Francesca? I know it's an exciting prospect, but I didn't think it was that good.'

Leaning forward, still grinning, she tapped him on the nose. 'You are a very clever man, Calum. And also very conniving. Do you think I don't see through this? What if I said I wanted to do it all, and not have Elaine's help?'

He smiled in acknowledgement of her perceptiveness. 'Then I would have to say that employing her company would be a condition of the job.'

'That's what I thought. I bet you've already promised it to her.' A rueful glint came into his eyes and she crowed with laughter. 'Calum, I'm beginning to think you've fallen for Elaine. Haven't you?'

'Me? No, of course not. You know I have to follow the family tradition and marry a blonde.'

She gave him a thoughtful look. 'So what are your intentions?' she ventured.

But that was going too far. Calum said, 'Do you want the job or don't you?'

'Of course I do; it will be fun.'

'Then you can start by arranging the celebrations we'll be holding in Madeira. Lennox's wife was going to organise them, but she's too pregnant, and Chris's mother really isn't interested in that kind of thing. So I've spoken to them both and they're more than happy to relinquish the task into your hands. Think you can manage that?'

'Yes, of course. When do you intend to hold them?'

'In less than two month's time.'

'In that case I'd better go out there straight away. I'll leave tomorrow.' She glanced out of the window, but her face was much more cheerful now. 'Let's hope the weather is better than this.'

It was. Madeira, with its ever temperate climate, was bathed in sunshine when her plane touched down the next day. Stella, her cousin Lennox's wife, was waiting at the airport to greet her. The two girls, both tall and fair, hugged each other but Stella's large bump got in the way, which made them burst out laughing.

'I'm so pleased you've come to take over,' Stella confided. 'I have a terrible dread of giving birth in the middle of one of the parties.'

They drove through Funchal to the big Brodey house outside the town, a house that used to be austere but which Stella had redecorated and turned into a warm, welcoming home. It was also an open house for any member of the family visiting the island, so Stella had naturally had a room prepared for Francesca. Lennox was away at the moment so, except for the staff, the two girls had the house to themselves. Francesca enjoyed the first couple of days, gossiping with Stella and taking over the arrangements for the celebrations. These were to be much more low-key here than in Oporto, because Brodey's had been established in Madeira for far longer than in Portugal. There were only going to be three large parties: one mainly for the benefit of foreign buyers who hadn't been able to make the celebrations in Oporto, another for local business contacts, and the third for the vineyard workers.

Francesca took over from Stella with ease, booking venues, writing out guest-lists and ordering invitations to be printed. But then Lennox came home and, although her cousin greeted her warmly and made her as welcome as Stella had, it was soon evident to Francesca that the two were completely wrapped up in one another and the coming birth of their child. Because she was one of the family, they didn't attempt to hide their feelings. Lennox would make excuses to come home from the office just to see Stella and make sure she was all right, and he would put his hand on her bump, feeling the child within, as they looked into each other's eyes, both their faces alight with love and tenderness. They were both so happy, Stella positively radiant.

Francesca was happy for them; she couldn't possibly be anything else. But seeing them together brought back only tormenting memories of her own unhappy marriage and deepened her wretchedness as she thought of her long, empty future. Finding that she couldn't bear it, she made the excuse that she needed to be in Funchal, and asked if she could move into the old Brodey house, behind the wine-lodge.

The house was a quiet oasis in the middle of the town, old and tranquil, its small garden hung with flame-coloured bougainvillaea and surrounded by a high wall that kept out the world. Stella drove her down there and they wandered round the house together.

'I lived here for a few weeks before we were married,' Stella said reminiscently, a smile curving her lips.

Glancing at her and the large four-poster bed in the room in which they stood, Francesca said, 'Is this where you and Lennox first...?'

But Stella shook her head. 'No, that was in the house on Porto Santo,' she said, mentioning the neighbouring island. Then she grinned. 'But we spent our wedding night in this bed.'

Francesca's eyebrows went up and she pretended to be shocked. 'Well, really! And I thought Lennox was so respectable.'

'He was—until I drove him to distraction.'

They both giggled as they went downstairs. Stella opened a bottle of wine and they took it out to the garden to drink, relaxing in comfortable garden chairs, enjoying the warmth of the sun and the scent of the flowers.

'Mmm, this is bliss,' Stella remarked.

'Yes,' Francesca agreed, but there was a catch in her voice that Stella immediately noticed.

Reaching across the table, she put her hand over Francesca's. 'I'm sorry,' she said. 'It must be tedious for you at the house. I'm afraid Lennox and I are rather wrapped up in each other and Lennox junior at the moment.'

'No, of course it's not tedious,' Francesca said quickly. 'I am just deeply, tremendously jealous of you, that's all.'

Stella looked startled. 'Of me?'

'Yes. Of what you have. A man who's crazy about you and whom you love in return. This baby that you both want so much. You're so happy, so perfectly happy.'

'Oh, please don't say that,' Stella said sharply, her hand suddenly tightening on Francesca's. 'Things always go wrong when you're too happy.'

'Nothing will go wrong,' Francesca reassured her swiftly. 'You'll be fine.'

'Sometimes I get scared,' Stella admitted. 'We both want this baby so much.' She was silent for a moment, fighting her fears, then remembered what Francesca had said. 'Before I was married, I would have envied you, your lifestyle. Jetting around all over the place, going to so many exciting parties, meeting people. But when I fell in love with Lennox I realised all that was just superficial, that the real quality of life was in loving someone and wanting to spend the rest of your life with that person. I'm sorry if seeing us together has made your lifestyle seem any the less attractive.'

'It's all I have,' Francesca said, reaching up to pick a spray of flowers from the bougainvillaea and twist them between her fingers.

'Was your marriage to Paolo so very bad?' Stella asked gently. 'He was very good-looking.'

Francesca gave a harsh laugh and her fingers tightened on the stem of the flowers, crushing it. 'His character didn't go with his looks. He turned out to be a pervert,' she said shortly.

'Oh, Francesca, I'm so sorry,' Stella said in horror. 'Did he—did he hurt you?'

Her face tightened. 'Sometimes. But mostly he preferred to humiliate me.' She bit her lip, thinking how different her own experience of marriage had been from that of the girl who sat beside her. Abruptly she changed the subject. 'I haven't been inside the wine-lodge for years. Will you show me round?'

They used the private door in the house that led to the old wine-lodge buildings, where the tourists came to sample the Madeira wine that the company produced on the island. There they found Lennox working in his office and he took little persuading to leave his work and take them both for a drive and to stop in a café overlooking the sea for lunch.

Francesca stayed in Funchal for another week, finalising what arrangements she could, sending out invitations, holding long conversations with Elaine over the phone. But when it got to the stage where she could do nothing more until nearer the time she flew to Paris for an orgy of shopping, then went on to Rome and did the same there. She also went to a lot of parties and other social events, picking up again with her high-flying friends. She spent a lot of time and money in casinos, went to the races, attended charity events; if there was a high-profile function going on anywhere in Europe, Francesca's name was invariably on the guest-list.

She also picked up again with men she had known, met some new ones and, as always, attracted many to her side. Photographs of her with some of her escorts appeared in magazines, and the gossip columnists latched on to her like leeches. A couple of the men showed great interest in her and were perfectly civilised, perfectly eligible, and tried to persuade her that they would be perfect lovers, too. Francesca flirted with them, just to stroke their egos, but soon grew bored and restless again. Nothing she did seemed to assuage that restlessness, and the thought of going to bed with either one was somehow repulsive.

Sooner than she need have done, Francesca went back to Madeira to prepare for the celebrations, staying again at the old house behind the wine-lodge. The acceptances had arrived and she began to make out seating plans, a task which was made rather difficult because Calum insisted on keeping a few places in reserve for buyers that he expected to invite almost at the last moment. But everything else went well; Elaine paid a flying visit to check on the arrangements and flew out again two days later, then the family began to arrive.

Chris's parents, who had their own villa on the island, arrived first, followed by Chris himself, who went to stay with them. Agog with curiosity, Francesca managed to get him at home alone one day and told him he could take her out for lunch in one of the little villages up in the hills.

'Do I have a choice?' he asked with a grin.

'Of course you don't. Come on, let's go.' And she got into the car that she'd borrowed from Lennox during her stay.

Francesca had often been to Madeira before, but never tired of its stupendous scenery: the high mountains falling into deep, deep ravines, the irrigation ditches called *levadas* which carried spring water down to villages and farms, so that the sweet sound of running water was always in the air.

They found a restaurant high up in the hills and sat at a table outside in the sun where they could look across to the peaks of the other mountains that surrounded them.

'I've been reading about you in the papers again,' Chris remarked.

'You couldn't have; there's been nothing to write about.'

'The gossip columns seem to think so. All these social events you've been attending, and your name linked with more eligible men.'

'I just went to Paris and Rome for a few weeks, that was all.'

'And the men?'

'What about them?'

'You know very well what I mean.'

She gave an impatient shrug. 'They were nothing, just escorted me to parties a couple of times.' Picking up the drink the waiter had brought, she looked at Chris over it. 'How about you? Have you been in New York since I saw you last?'

'Most of the time, aside from a few business trips now and again.'

'What about Tiffany?'

Immediately he closed up. 'What about her?'

Parodying his earlier words, Francesca said, 'You know very well what I mean.'

That made him grin, but he wasn't very forthcoming, merely saying, 'She's still with me.'

'I thought you'd have grown tired of her by now,' Francesca ventured.

He looked away and she saw his hand tighten on his glass. 'No.'

Probing carefully, she said, 'It would be a big mistake to fall in love with Tiffany.'

His eyes came up to meet hers. 'Can falling in love ever be a mistake?'

'If you fall in love with the wrong person, yes.'

'Was Paolo the wrong person?' Chris asked, deliberately being cruel.

She flinched, but said, 'Yes, of course he was. I married him too quickly. I didn't give myself time to find out that it was only the marriage I wanted and not the man. I wouldn't like you to make the same kind of mistake, Chris. It—hurts too much. When you're vulnerable it's like a living hell.'

'But if it was the right person,' he said slowly, 'wouldn't it then be like heaven?'

'Do you feel that way about Tiffany?'

But Chris frowned as he said, 'For some reason she won't open up with me. She never talks about her family or her past.'

'Why would she, if it's shady?'

'If she trusted me she would. I think that trust is very important in a relationship, almost as important as love. Don't you?'

'I suppose so.'

Her voice sounded a little offhand, making Chris look at her with a frown. After a moment, he said, 'Have you heard from Sam Gallagher?'

Francesca picked up her sunglasses and put them on. 'This sun is so strong,' she remarked. 'Who? Oh, you mean the American who was in Oporto. No, I wouldn't expect to. Why? Have you?'

Chris, watching her keenly, shook his head. 'No.'

Looking out across the mountain-tops, Francesca said, 'I expect he went back to his cows and his log-cabin. Going to Portugal was probably the big adventure of his life, a story to tell his children and his grandchildren: The day I went to Portugal and met a princess,' she said, mimicking a narrative style.

'Shouldn't it be fell in love with a princess?'

Her head swung round. 'Don't be ridiculous.'

'I thought he was pretty gone on you. So did Calum.'

'You were mistaken,' she said stiffly.

'Why don't you go to the States and look him up?'

'I've got better things to do.'

'Such as getting your name in the papers and going around with men who bore you, I suppose?' Francesca was about to deny it hotly, but before she could do so Chris added, 'One thing about Sam—he was never boring.'

She realised almost with surprise that it was true, and fell silent, not speaking again until their food was served, then keeping to the safe subject of the future celebrations.

The first of these was imminent and Francesca was kept busy over the next few days, meeting guests at the airport and ferrying them either to the Brodey house or to their hotel. Grandfather arrived, but her mother rang to say that she had a bad cold and wouldn't be coming, which meant her father wouldn't come either. As Chris's mother was to be the official hostess in Madeira, their absence made little difference.

Calum arrived from Portugal almost immediately after Elaine had flown in from England with her team of helpers, which Francesca found interesting. But the two of them behaved quite emotionlessly towards each other, as far as Francesca could tell. But then, neither Elaine nor Calum was the kind of person to let her or his feelings show in public.

The day before the first celebration party, Francesca went to the airport again to meet some of Calum's last-minute guests whose names she didn't even know. Calum had merely sent her a message giving the times of the flights and telling her to meet five guests and take them to their hotel in Funchal. So she went to the airport in the company minibus, the driver holding up a sign with 'BRODEY' written on it when they reached the concourse.

The first couple, a representative of a British company and his wife, arrived on time, but they had to wait some twenty minutes for the other three guests. The next two, another married couple, were from America, from Oregon, the owners of a chain of stores which sold the Brodey wines. Francesca greeted them warmly, enquired about their flight, introduced them to the other couple, and so it was a few minutes before she was able to look round for her fifth guest.

She saw him at once. Sam Gallagher. Walking purposefully across the concourse towards them. So tall and broad; so suddenly and achingly familiar that her heart did a crazy flip and she couldn't move, couldn't breathe.

He came up to them quickly, giving her no time to recover from her surprise, his eyes on her face, intent and searching. He didn't smile, for a moment didn't speak, not until Francesca dropped her eyes, petrified by her own emotions, by the huge surge of gladness that had filled her heart. Then he said a little drily, 'Hello, Francesca.'

'S-Sam.' She licked lips which weren't quite steady.

He put out a hand to take hers but she pretended not to see it and turned away, saying brightly, 'Well, now we're all here, let's go out to the car. You're sure you have all your luggage?'

The others assured her that they had and she led the way out to the bus.

She sat in the front passenger seat during the drive to the town and took no part in the conversation going on in the back until the American woman asked her some questions about the island and she had to answer. But even then she managed not to look directly at Sam. By now she had recovered a little and begun to feel angry at the way this had been sprung on her, at the way she'd been set up. Whose idea had it been? she wondered, beginning to seethe. Calum's? Chris's? Or had it been Sam who had somehow been able to persuade one of them to invite him?

She would have liked to demand an answer from Sam right now, to face up to him and *make* him tell her. But she had to be polite and friendly until they reached the hotel because of the other guests. Then she had to see that they were checked in and given their itinerary for the few days of their stay. But there was no booking for Sam at the hotel and he didn't follow her into it. When she emerged he had got out of the bus and was leaning against its side, hands in his pockets, completely casual.

'Which hotel are you booked into?' Francesca said sharply.

'I'm not. I've been invited to stay at the house with the family.'

She stared at him, realising the implications, realising that all three of her cousins must have connived at this. Perhaps even Stella, too.

'The driver will take you, then,' she said shortly.

'Aren't you coming?'

'No. I'm not staying there,' she told him on a note of triumph and relief.

'Can't we give you a lift somewhere?'

'No. I'm staying in the town; I can walk there.'

'Then I'll walk with you,' Sam returned. And he turned to speak to the driver, telling him to go on to the house.

The driver looked at Francesca for corroboration, and she hesitated, knowing that she'd much rather be alone to get over the shock of seeing Sam here, to work out what her attitude towards him was going to be. But it seemed that Sam was determined to stay with her, and she knew him well enough to know that she couldn't just order him to get back on the bus, because he wouldn't go. So she gave the driver a reluctant nod and he drove away.

When he'd gone, Francesca felt strangely vulnerable, very much alone. Sam looked at her averted face for a moment, then said, 'Is there anywhere round here where we can get a drink? Not the hotel—a café or something?'

'This way.'

She led him through the town to a street leading down to the sea, where numerous cafés had tables set out on the pavement under colourful umbrellas. It was a pedestrian zone so was comparatively quiet, the noise of traffic a distant hum, as was the sound of the waves breaking on the shore. They sat down and Sam ordered a Campari for her, a beer for himself.

'It's good to see you again,' he said as soon as the waiter had gone.

She turned a pair of blazing grey eyes on him. 'Just whose idea was it?' she demanded.

'Does it matter?'

'Yes, it darn well does. Because I have a great deal to say to whoever arranged this,' she said bitterly.

'Say it to me, then,' Sam answered coolly.

Cornered, given no time to think, to test her own emotions, Francesca could only fall back on her previous decision, and on anger. For a moment she glared at him, then said hotly, 'You're wasting your time coming here, Sam. I've already given you my answer—I'm not interested.'

His lids lowered in one of his lazy smiles. 'Aren't you jumping the gun?'

'What do you mean?'

'What makes you think I've come here because of you?' She looked at him, waiting for him to go on. 'I'm here because I've bought an interest in a wine company and got invited for the celebrations.'

'I don't believe you,' she said flatly.

He shrugged his wide shoulders. 'Ask Calum, then.'

'I won't believe him either.'

That made him grin, the first time he'd smiled, and her heart gave that idiotic jerk again. He seemed a little more tanned than he had been back in Oporto, but otherwise he was completely and devastatingly the same as she remembered, the same as the memory that had too often filled her thoughts during the last months. The force of her feelings frightened her again.

She said shortly, 'You can get a cab to the Brodey house. All of the drivers will know where the estate is.'

She went to get up but Sam caught her wrist and made her stay in her seat. Pulling his chair close to hers, he said, 'Why so agitated, Francesca? Why, if you really don't care about me?'

'I'm just angry, that's all. You—Calum—you had no right to do this. But I couldn't care less about you.'

'Isn't there some sort of quotation about protesting too much? I think you're lying, Francesca. I think you're afraid.'

'Of you?' She laughed scornfully. 'No way.'

'Not of me, of your own feelings.' He put a hand on her neck and his voice softened. 'You might as well admit it, because you gave yourself away when you saw me back at the airport—until you tried to hide it. But I *know* how you feel, and I'm not going to let you deny it again.'

She stared into his eyes, completely overwhelmed, unable to think. His hand tightened and Sam began to draw her to him, his eyes darkening. Realising that he was going to kiss her, right here in the middle of town, she stiffened and her eyes became angry again. 'Don't you dare!'

But that was the wrong thing to say. A gleam came into Sam's eyes and his arm went round her.

'No!' She put her hands against his chest, but knew that it would do little good. 'Not here, Sam, *please*,' she said urgently.

'Not *here*?' He raised an eyebrow but relaxed his hold a little. She shook her head, looking at him pleadingly. After a moment he let her go and said, 'OK, so let's finish our drinks, shall we?'

Francesca picked up her untouched drink, concentrated on it, wished it had been a beer so that it would have lasted ten times as long. For a while they were silent, then she lifted a strained face to look at him. 'You shouldn't have come here, Sam.' But there was no anger left in her voice, just a sort of deep regret, almost sadness.

He reached to take her hand, but she put it quickly in her lap. His tone firm, almost fierce, he said, 'You're wrong. And I'm going to prove it to you.' Their eyes met and held for a long moment, then Sam, easing the tension, confident that he had made his point, sat back and said, 'This looks a real nice place. I'm sure looking forward to seeing as much of the island as I can.'

She accepted the change of subject with intense gratitude and was able to answer him automatically, to push her chaotic thoughts and emotions temporarily below the surface. When they'd finished their drinks, she took him to a cab rank.

'When will I see you?' he demanded.

'Tomorrow night, I suppose, at the party for all the guests.'

'What about tonight?'

She shook her head. 'It's the dinner for the locals tonight. There's a cocktail party laid on for all the other guests at the hotel this evening; you should go to that.'

'I want to see you,' he said urgently.

Again she shook her head, gave the direction to the driver, then stepped back. Sam's face hardened for a moment, then he got in the car and it sped away.

Francesca watched until it was out of sight as it rounded a corner, then turned and began to hurry to the old Brodey house. She let herself in and went into the garden, to sit on the stone seat beneath the acacia tree, her legs up on the seat and her arms tightly round her bent knees. She felt vulnerable and afraid. Her thoughts were a jumbled mess. It was true that she'd often thought of Sam since they'd been apart, and had felt lonely and restless, but nothing had prepared her for the fistful of emotions that had hit her when she'd seen him walking towards her at the airport. She tried to define, to rationalise her feelings, but couldn't. They were a crazy tumult of excitement, fear, joy, dread, anger and cowardice— the latter because she was more than half inclined to get on the first plane out of Madeira, to run away from Sam and from these emotions, because she was too afraid to face up to either.

Francesca had never thought of herself as a coward before, and to realise now that she wanted to run away greatly alarmed her. She put her hands on her head, gripping her hair till it hurt, trying to force herself to think clearly. OK, so what if Sam had come here? She'd turned him down once and she could do it again. If he asked her. If he still wanted to marry her. But why else would he have come?

For a lax moment Francesca wondered what it would be like to be married to Sam, to live in Wyoming on a cattle ranch, to have him make love to her every night in a big wooden bed with a patchwork quilt that his grandmother had probably made. Her eyes softened, until she thought of the long days when he would be away, branding and rounding up, or whatever cowboys had to do. To be alone like that would, she was certain, drive her mad. The whole idea was ridiculous: she could never live that kind of life, and it would end up making them both miserable.

Foreseeing a future involving another marriage break-up, another painful divorce, Francesca knew that she had to continue to be strong, to deny the surging excitement of seeing Sam again, and not let things go any further. All right, then, so emotions weren't to be allowed into it; that was decided. But what if he should kiss her again, the way he had before?

Immediately, at just the thought, her heart began to pound. But that's just physical chemistry, she told herself sternly. Call it lust, if you like. And in this day and age lust doesn't have to compute with marriage, and definitely not with love.

But how to persuade Sam to see it that way? He would appear to be an upright man, one of traditional values, although she was willing to bet that he was far from inexperienced. So why take this moralistic attitude with her, of all people? She could think of only one reason—the one Sam had given her himself: it was because he was in love with her, because he wanted it to be for keeps and not a cheap affair. A flash of anger lit her eyes as Francesca thought that an affair with her would never be *cheap*!

It came to her that it would be a lot better for both of them if they could just go to bed together and get this out of their systems. If Sam got serious again she would tell him so, and if he wouldn't agree—well, she would just have to seduce him.

That thought brought a curving smile to her lips. Yet again she remembered the explosive embraces they had exchanged back in Oporto, but this time she let the ache of frustration take over instead of trying to fight it. The fierce urgency of need filled her body and there was only one way to fulfil it and one man who could give her what she wanted—whether he liked it or not.

Tomorrow night, she thought. Tomorrow night, after the party, I'll get Sam alone and I'll *make* him make love to me.

CHAPTER SEVEN

IT WAS in a state of volatile excitement that Francesca got ready for the party the following night. But she dressed carefully, putting on a dress of shimmering blue silk, taking time to make sure that she looked good. Usually for an occasion like this she wore her hair up, but tonight she brushed it loose, letting it fall to her shoulders in a thick golden mane. She knew it made her look younger and less elegant that way, less sophisticated; she hoped it would also make her look more—approachable? Hardly the right word for what she had in mind: she was going to make sure that Sam got a whole lot closer than that.

She had seen him twice more since he'd arrived on the island, although she hadn't expected to. He had been in the car with Calum and Chris when Calum had driven down to the old house last night to collect her and take her to the dinner for the local businessmen and their wives at Reid's hotel, a little way outside Funchal on the coast. Chris had been sitting in the front passenger seat and had got out to hold the rear door open for her.

Francesca, recovering from seeing Sam with them, had given Chris a brittle smile as she'd walked up, and said menacingly, 'I shall have words with you two later.'

He grinned. 'I'm only surprised you haven't already. We've been living in fear and trembling all afternoon.'

Francesca gave him a look and got into the back seat.

Sam's eyes swept her face, checking on her mood, probably, an eyebrow rising in surprise when she greeted

143

him with apparent calm. Calum, too, seemed surprised. He looked over the seat, appeared to be about to say something, but, seeing the challenge in her eyes, thought better of it and drove on.

Sam was wearing an ordinary suit, not a dinner-jacket, but she still said, 'Are you going to the businessmen's dinner?'

'No. I'm going to borrow Calum's car, see something of the island before it gets dark.'

Francesca gave a small sigh of relief; she had been wondering if she might have to bring her plans forward a day, and she was glad she didn't: a girl liked to be fully prepared when she set out to seduce a man.

Reaching out, Sam lightly touched her arm. An immediate *frisson* of awareness ran through her; his touch seemed to burn into her skin like the branding-irons he must use in his work. Controlling herself with an effort, she turned her head to look at him. She had intended to give him a cool, rather aloof kind of glance, but what she saw in his eyes made every other thought fade away. He gazed at her steadily, letting her see how he felt. There was admiration for her beauty, and warmth, and tenderness. The darkness of desire was there too, and a hint of sensuality, but most of all his eyes were intense with love—a love he wasn't afraid to show.

She gazed at him for a long, long moment in which time seemed to stand still, taken aback by the openness of the emotions he was letting her see. But then she frowned and looked away, down into her lap, her hands gripped together.

They were soon at the hotel and Francesca didn't even look at Sam again, walking straight inside when the door was opened for her. But, although she behaved outwardly with her usual warmth and charm to their guests that evening, Francesca's mind was far away from the party. She answered her neighbours mechanically, but her disturbed thoughts were on Sam.

She saw him again the next morning when she had to go up to the house to finalise the arrangements for the party there with Elaine. The family house wasn't large enough for the three hundred or so guests who had been invited so they had hired a huge marquee which had been erected in the grounds. Elaine was busy supervising the swaths of flowers that were being placed on the tall poles which held up the roof of the tent, and Sam was halfway up a ladder, helping the workman who was doing the job.

Luckily, Francesca saw him first and paused only a moment before leaving the marquee, determined to avoid him if she could because she didn't want Sam to have an opportunity to propose to her again.

Outside, she bumped into Calum, who put his hands on her shoulders to steady her.

'Why did you invite Sam?' she asked abruptly.

His brows flickered for a moment, then he said, 'Because you were restless, and seemed hell-bent on self-destruction. Because Sam kept phoning me to ask how you were. Because I——'

'All right,' she broke in. 'I get the picture.'

'Are you pleased?'

She raised uncertain eyes to his. 'I'll let you know.'

She avoided Sam for the rest of the day and he didn't come looking for her, which rather surprised her.

But now she would have to face him. Francesca gave a last look at her reflection; she had done her best, and if she couldn't seduce Sam tonight... But she resolutely pushed such a pessimistic thought out of her mind and went to the party.

Again she saw Sam before he saw her. He was with Chris and Calum, standing in the large hall of the house, all of them wearing evening suits, all three tall and good-looking. Francesca had just come from seeing Elaine in the marquee, and walked into the hall from the back of the building. Calum saw her and his eyes widened as he took in the beautiful, clinging dress and her swirl of hair. Following his gaze, the other two looked round, and she had the satisfaction of seeing Sam give a small gasp as he stared at her. Chris might have reacted too, but she didn't notice.

Walking towards her, Sam took her hands in his, his eyes again full of that emotion he had for her alone. He shook his head, as if lost for words. 'You look—just stunning,' he said on a note of wonderment.

She didn't respond too much, just gave him a small smile and took her hands away as she saw Grandfather and Chris's parents coming down the stairs to join them.

The members of the family split up for dinner, each of them sitting at a different table, and Francesca had made sure that Sam wasn't on hers. There were several reasons for this: she didn't want the danger of getting into an argument with him, of having to put him off if he came on strong, and also because she knew she wouldn't be able to concentrate on being an attentive host to the other diners if he was there—his presence was too disturbing.

After the meal, though, they all circulated round the tables, talking generally to the guests until everyone quietened as they watched an exhibition of folk-dancing by islanders in traditional costume. The men wore white with red cummerbunds and waistcoats, the women red and yellow striped skirts and red bolero jackets, with bright red capes hanging from one shoulder. It was

pleasant to watch and gave everyone a chance to rest
after the meal and the wine.

The folk-dancers filed out on a long roll of applause,
a band started to play for everyone to dance, and Sam
was immediately by her side. 'I've let you take care of
the other guests for long enough,' he told her. 'Now it's
my turn.' Leading her on to the floor, he drew her to
him, not too close, but close enough for Francesca's heart
to go a little faster. But she played it cool at first, asking
him how he'd spent his day, what he thought of the
island.

'It's a fascinating place,' he said sincerely. 'I thought
the Douro valley was beautiful, but Madeira is—well,
just magnificent. And so green. I thought a volcanic
island would be black and barren, but here it's like a
huge garden, full of flowers and vines.'

'Did you go to one of our vineyards?'

'There wasn't time.' He gave her a contemplative,
almost wary look, and said, 'Why don't you take me to
see one tomorrow?'

He spoke as if he expected a refusal, but she hardly
hesitated before nodding and saying, 'Yes, OK.' His eyes,
alight with pleasure, came quickly to her face, but before
he could speak she said, 'I'm surprised that you were
able to get away from your work again so soon after
your trip to Portugal.'

'When Calum invited me here and told me you were
coming, nothing would have kept me away,' he said
simply.

She gave him a disturbed look, wondering if he was
spending all his money on these trips. Her hand was on
his shoulder and as she ran her fingers over the cloth it
occurred to her that it was of very good quality, that the
suit was well-made. She realised, too, that although Sam

dressed casually he didn't dress cheaply. Slowly she raised her eyes and met his quizzical gaze. 'You're not just a ranch-hand, are you?'

'I do own the ranch,' he admitted. 'I could take care of you, Francesca.'

She looked at him for a moment, a frown in her eyes, then said abruptly, 'I'm tired of this party. Let's leave.'

Her car was outside, parked where it wouldn't be obstructed by other vehicles. Sam took off his jacket and tossed it in the back, then got in the passenger seat and let Francesca take the wheel. She had intended to take him back to the old house, to the room with the four-poster bed, but when she reached the gates and the road she suddenly turned in the other direction and headed up into the hills. She drove fast in the moonlight, over-steering on the steep bends so that the tyres protested when she braked hard, revving too much so that the engine screamed.

Sam, not at all afraid, said, 'Do you mind telling me where we're going?'

'You said you hadn't seen a vineyard; I'm taking you to one.'

'They look better in the dark, do they?'

The wryness in his voice brought a quirk of amusement to her lips and she slowed down a little, glanced at him. Sam was leaning back in his seat, his eyes half closed, apparently happy to put his trust in her, in her driving ability. It was a trust that was well-placed because she was a good driver and knew her way round these roads which wound, with hairpin bends, up into the mountains. But it rather annoyed her that she hadn't scared him.

A determined look came into Francesca's eyes. She threw the car round a bend and hurtled straight at the solid wall of the mountain, only braking and turning the car with a shriek of protesting tyres and engine at the last possible second. Again she looked at Sam. He was grinning. The darn man was grinning! He was enjoying it.

When he saw her expression of chagrin he burst out laughing. 'I've done some rally-driving in my time.'

'In mountains?'

'In mountains,' he agreed with a nod.

The lights of an oncoming car pierced the darkness. Francesca slowed down to pass it and didn't attempt to pick up so much speed again. She ought to have known he wouldn't be afraid; he looked as if he'd never been afraid of anything.

She took a side-turning and drove for another half-mile before she came to the gates of one of the Brodey vineyards, but instead of going through them she went on along the road a little way and turned up a dirt track that came to an end on a small plateau of land on the side of the mountain. Getting out of the car, they walked to the edge. The light from the moon was so strong, it was like a weirdly colourless, silvered daylight. By it, they saw that spread out all around them as far as they could see, on every slope, however steep, were thousand upon thousand rows of vines.

'This is it,' Francesca said simply.

Sam whistled incredulously. 'All this belongs to Brodey's?'

'Yes. The workers live in those little white houses with thatched roofs that are dotted around the hills.'

'They must be like mountain goats to keep their balance on these slopes,' Sam commented.

'Yes, I suppose they are.'

'That water I can hear—is that one of the irrigation channels I read about?'

'Yes, they're called *levadas*. They bring fresh spring water down from the mountains.'

They were silent for a few minutes, listening, taking in the incredible view. Then Sam turned, reached for her and said, 'Francesca?' on a soft note.

It was the perfect setting for romance, for deep, tender kisses, for another declaration of love, another proposal of marriage. But Francesca didn't want that. In a sudden fit of caprice, perhaps mixed with apprehension, she kicked off her high heels and ran through the soft dry soil to the edge of the plateau. 'Come and see the vines,' she called, and jumped off the edge to the first terrace.

'Francesca!' Sam's voice was sharp with consternation. He came after her, fast, saw that she was only a few feet below him and jumped down beside her. Almost before he'd landed he'd taken her by the shoulders and was shaking her. 'You crazy little fool! I didn't know it was safe,' he yelled at her—and she realised that there was something of which Sam was afraid, after all.

But she just laughed on a high-pitched note and pulled him along with her. 'Come and taste the grapes.'

She ran down the row of waist-high vines, found a full bunch of dark grapes, fat and shining in the moonlight. 'These are the best grapes, the noble grapes,' she told him, pulling some of them off. 'Here, taste them.'

She pushed two of them into his mouth, watched as he bit into them, then reached up to kiss him fiercely before he could swallow them down. The juice was on his lips, pungent on his tongue. She could taste it on her own mouth, on her own tongue as it probed and found his. Sam gave a muffled exclamation of mingled sur-

prise and delight. His arms went round her and he tried
to hold her tight against him, but Francesca broke free.
Her eyes wide and hungry, she put another grape half
in her mouth, then came close so that he could bite into
the other half.

The juice, still warm from the day's sun, sweet beyond
compare, spurted into their mouths, ran down their
chins. Putting out her tongue, still stained red, Francesca
delicately wiped the tip along the trail of juice that ran
down his jaw and throat, the touch feather-light, sensual,
teasing—the most tantalising moment he had ever
known. Sam groaned, the sound hoarse and thick, and
his fingers tightened as he held her.

She crammed more grapes into his mouth, into her
own, kissing him as they ate, the juice staining their
mouths. Sharing the grapes, crushing them against each
other's lips as they kissed greedily, eagerly, their breath
hot and panting, both of them were lost now to anything
but the sensuality of those avid kisses.

As she made small animal noises of need, Francesca's
hands went to his tie, pulled it off, and tore open the
buttons of his shirt. She grabbed at some more grapes
and crushed them hard against his chest, on his nipples
and the mat of dark hairs between. Then she lowered
her head to lick them off. Her breath was burning hot
against his skin; the softness of her lips and the rapa-
cious possessiveness of her tongue roused Sam to a fever
pitch of excitement. He gave a groaning cry, his head
thrown back, his hold so fierce that he bruised her arms.
He tried to speak but her head came up and she took
his mouth again, her grape-stained hands on either side
of his head, kissing him in a fever of desire.

Something seemed to erupt inside Sam. His hands went
to the back of her dress, searching for a fastening, but,

finding none, he dragged it from her shoulders, tearing
it in his haste, pulling it down to her waist. Then he
crushed her against him, as hard as she had crushed the
grapes, held her there as he gave himself up to the joy
of feeling her skin against his own, the heat of her, the
delightful roundness of her breasts titillating his overwhelming yearning.

Locked in each other's arms, they staggered a little,
stumbled, found themselves on their knees, still wrapped
in that close embrace, lost now in the shadows of the
vines. Sam's hand was on her breast, hot and shaking
with excitement, then his lips, greedily taking her small,
hard nipple, driving her so wild that she too cried out
her frustrated desire, her hands in his hair, finding it too
delightful to bear but never wanting it to stop. His lips
sucked, pulled, tightened, until she couldn't stand it any
longer and pushed him away with a cry.

He let her go, gasping, his breath unsteady with trembling excitement. For a moment they stared into each
other's eyes, almost unable to believe the erotic wonder
of what they were doing to each other. Reaching out,
Sam put both hands on her breasts, leaving smears of
dust and juice. Francesca gave a long, low moan as he
slowly caressed her, as she moved voluptuously within
his cupped hands. His eyes on her face, his own excitement increased as he saw the pleasure he was giving
her.

Suddenly she fell against him and the next moment
they were on the ground, kissing again, almost fighting
in their eagerness, each of them now tearing at the other's
clothes as they rolled down the hillside among the vines.
Stalks broke, tendrils caught at their hair, the rich smell
of earth and leaves was in their nostrils, whole bunches
of grapes were crushed under them, between them. Juice

mingled with the dust and caked their backs, their legs and thighs.

The sound of water came very close, and as they both dragged off Sam's last piece of clothing they rolled on to the grass path that followed the course of the *levada* down the mountainside. The fragrance of a nearby jacaranda tree, the scent of the bruised grass beneath them were a potent aphrodisiac that could only increase their passion.

Francesca was now partly lying on Sam. She lifted herself fully over him, biting, kissing, licking, moving her legs along the length of his, her stomach against the hard plane of his thighs, her breasts brushing his chest.

Sam's hoarse, breathless groans were loud in her ears. His body was burning hot and slippery with the sweat and excitement and anticipation. She could taste it on his skin, on his lips when he put his hand in her hair and dragged her head up so that he could kiss her with ravenous hunger. All of a sudden he swung her beneath him and Francesca gave a cry as she felt the cold water and the clean cement bed of the *levada* on her back. The water was shallow, only a couple of inches deep, but it ran swiftly, taking her hair and spreading it around her head like a halo in the rippling water, sending small waves and splashes along the length of her burning skin.

Suddenly, it seemed a fitting place for love, this living bed turned to molten silver in the moonlight, among the verdant vines and the exotic scent of the night. Sam raised himself over her, looked down at her for a moment, his face taut with need, his breath a broken, shuddering sigh of aching anticipation. Then he came down on her, taking her with the fierce passion and impatient hunger that was right for this place, right after the erotic embraces that had led to it, right for the kind

of man he was and the kind of woman under him. It
was inflamed, primitive, unforgettable, lifting them both
to the height of rapture.

Sam's great long groan of gasping pleasure filled the
air, drowning out her own shuddering moans. His taut,
stretched body slowly relaxed and he sank down at her
side. Putting his arm under her head, lifting it clear of
the water, he kissed her, his breath still uneven, and
murmured broken words of love, gratitude, wonder. He
kissed her eyes, smoothed the tentacles of wet hair from
her face with a hand that was still shaking.

'Oh, God, sweetheart. So wonderful—so wonderful.
Oh, my darling girl.'

Francesca was too exhausted to do anything but lie
back in his arms. Her eyes were closed but there was a
look of wonder in her face, the curve of an ecstatic smile
on her lips. Her heart hadn't yet slowed and it seemed
as if her breath would never get back to normal. But it
was heaven to lie in Sam's arms, to hear all the wonderful things he was saying to her.

But presently she grew chill. Sam stood up and lifted
her to her feet. He kissed her and said huskily, 'Honey,
we've got to find a bed.'

The water had washed most of the dust off her but
Sam's back was still covered in that and juice, so she
made him turn round and used her hands to scoop up
the water and wash him. She did so without haste, enjoying the freedom to rove his body, to marvel at the
width of his shoulders, run her fingers down his spine,
across the pale skin of his rounded buttocks, and down
the long, long length of his strong, muscular legs.

'There, you're clean,' she said softly.

Sam turned round, a boyish, rueful grin on his face.

For a moment she didn't understand, then glanced down. 'Oh, Sam!' She smiled. 'You know that saying about Texas? Well, it's wrong: Wyoming definitely has the biggest and the best!'

He gave a shout of laughter, then put his hands on her waist to lift her above him and swing her round. 'Francesca, Francesca, Francesca!' He shouted her name into the night. 'You've made me the happiest man in the whole wide world.'

She laughed down at him, her hands on his shoulders. 'And will again, I hope.'

'Oh, yes. Oh, yes.' His eyes darkened with desire as he looked at her silken body, glistening like marble in the moonlight. His hands tightened, and she gasped in stunned surprise as he lowered her down on to his shafting manhood.

Later, when they came to dress, they couldn't find several bits of clothing. Francesca's dress was too torn for her to put on anyway, so she had to settle for her shoes, Sam's smeared shirt sarong-style round her waist, and his jacket. Which didn't leave him with much. They found his trousers without difficulty but couldn't find his underpants or one shoe. They got back in the car, overcome with laughter at the way they were dressed, so different from the civilised couple who'd arrived there.

'You look like the cat that got the cream,' Sam remarked, kissing her nose.

'I did! I did! And you look as if you had a whole jug of milk too,' she said, seeing the big, contented grin on Sam's face. They kissed again, but then Francesca said reluctantly, 'We'd better get back; it must be dawn soon. What's the time?'

Sam peered at his watch. 'I don't know; I think it must have stopped.' She went to switch on the engine, but he said, 'Just a minute. There's something I've just gotta do.' And, parting his jacket, he revealed her rosy-tipped breasts, stroked them with his fingertips until the nipples hardened, then bent to kiss them.

When he straightened Francesca's head was tilted back, her eyes closed and mouth pouting open in sexual awareness.

Seeing her like that, Sam said in husky urgency, 'Let's get back, sweetheart.'

She opened her eyes, looking into his face, and gunned the engine. But when they reached the town he had to crouch down in his seat in case there were any police about who might see his bare chest, which made Francesca giggle.

'Stop it,' he told her in mock-sternness. 'If we were arrested now your family would never forgive me.'

But they reached the old house safely. Francesca drove in and closed the gates, then took him up to her room.

They showered first, sharing it without question, washing off the last of the grime and the grape-juice that still stained their skin. Then Sam towelled her dry, making a very thorough job of it, and carried her to the bed. She waited for him to join her, knowing that they would make love again. And this time, although there was as much passion as before, it wasn't so wild, so primitive. They took it slowly, wanting to please each other now, using their combined knowledge and experience to lift the other to the heights of sensual excitement, to prolong it until at last they lay exhausted and fell immediately asleep in the closest embrace.

When they woke it was full light, the sun's rays shafting through a gap in the curtains. Sam moved and Francesca woke to find that they were both lying on their left side, Sam's arms around her as he held her close and safe. He murmured something, moved a little, and the next second they were making love once more.

Francesca fell asleep again and this time woke to the smell of coffee. She sat up and Sam handed her a mug from the tray he'd placed on the bedside table. 'I won't say good morning—we already did that in the greatest possible way,' he murmured, leaning forward to kiss her. 'Nice place you've got here,' he added, leaning back.

'It's attached to the wine-lodge. The family used to live here before they moved out of the town.'

'Are we likely to be disturbed—a cleaner or someone?'

'No, not today.'

'Then how do you feel about spending the day right here?'

She smiled and looked at him over her mug. 'It was good, wasn't it?'

'No,' he said emphatically, making Francesca raise her eyebrows. 'It was magnificent. The best.' Reaching out, he picked up her hand and kissed it. 'Thank you for last night, my darling. It was...' he paused as he sought for the right words '...it was the night of my nights,' he finished simply.

She smiled, liking that. Finishing her coffee, Francesca set the mug down, then leaned back against the wooden bedhead, still feeling drowsy from the physical excess of so much love.

The sheet had slipped down and she found Sam looking at her as he said huskily, 'You must hurry up and set a date for our wedding, my darling, because I can't wait to get you home and have you all to myself.'

That made her open her eyes wide. Sitting up straighter, she said, 'Aren't you jumping the gun, Sam?'

He grinned. 'So you want an official proposal, do you?' Setting down his mug, he took hold of her hands, his eyes deeply tender and loving. 'In that case, my beautiful, wonderful girl, *my* princess, I can only tell you that I love you with all my heart and I'll go on loving you until the day I die. So will you come to me and be my wife?' His mouth creased into a happy smile as he let go of one of her hands to gently touch her breast. 'And I must say, honey, that you are hardly in a position to say no.'

Taking her hand from his, Francesca covered herself with the sheet and drew her knees up to rest her chin on them. Her face averted, she said, 'I already told you I'm not looking for marriage, Sam.'

The expectant look in his eyes faded. Then he said, 'But you knew that was what I wanted. And you must have realised that I came to Madeira to try to persuade you to change your mind. Didn't you, Francesca?'

She gave a reluctant nod. 'Yes, I suppose so.'

'So what was the idea of taking me out to the vineyard, of letting me make love to you, if you weren't ready to marry me?'

'I felt the same way as I did back in Oporto. I was attracted to you; I wanted to go to bed with you.' She made a sharp, cutting gesture with her hand. 'But that doesn't mean I want to commit myself to you for the rest of my life.'

'So just what does it mean?' Sam demanded, his voice tightening.

'It was good, Sam; it can be again. Let's leave it at that.'

'No, I won't damn well leave it like that!' Suddenly angry, he caught her wrist and made her look at him. 'What's this supposed to be—a cheap one-night stand?'

'No!'

'What, then? A few days together here and there over the years if we happen to meet up?'

Francesca looked uncomfortable. 'Well, yes, I suppose so.'

Something close to disgust came into Sam's eyes. 'And that's all my love means to you, does it? I offer you my life and all you want is a few days of sex whenever you feel the need—or whenever there's no one else available,' he added with self-inflicted pain.

Francesca flinched. 'I didn't mean it like that.'

'How, then?'

'We could meet up often. I could come and stay with you, and you could come to Oporto or Rome, or wherever. Whenever we have the time. We could—we could be loving friends.'

Gritting his teeth, Sam said, 'I don't want a friend. I want a wife, someone to share my life, *all* of it. And I want kids.' His hands balling into fists, he said curtly, 'And having some classy mistress who spares time for me now and again sure as hell wouldn't make up for losing all of that!'

Francesca gulped, then broke the tenseness by saying, 'Then I'm sorry, Sam, but I'm not the one for you.'

'Yes, you damn well are.' Suddenly he was on his knees, forgetful of his nakedness, and had gripped her shoulders to shake her. 'You know it's right between us. Can you deny that you love me? Can you?' Again he shook her.

Putting up weak hands to hold him off, Francesca cried out unhappily, 'Sam, don't. Please!'

'No! I'm going to make you admit it. I'm going to make you say that you love me, that you'll marry me,' he said vehemently, his voice rising as he tried to force his will on her.

'No, I can't!' With a great effort she pushed him away. 'I *can't* marry you!'

'Can't?' He sat back on his heels, staring at her. But she had turned away, put her head in her hands. Sam strove to control himself, then said, 'Why not, Francesca?'

She didn't answer for a moment, then lifted a strained face, but still didn't look at him as she said, 'Because I'm too afraid.'

'Afraid of me?' Sam asked in an appalled voice.

'No, of—of love, of marriage.' With difficulty she explained, 'I've only really been in love once bef—once in my life, when I was nineteen and at college in America. But he—he just walked out on me, out of my life. Didn't say goodbye, nothing. I never heard from him again. And I didn't know why. I still don't. I was—was completely devastated. I failed my exams, dropped out of college; I lost all confidence in myself. Then I met Paolo and he kept telling me how much he loved me, so I told myself I was in love with him.' She lifted an unsteady hand to push her hair from her face. 'But he—he became cruel. Maybe it was my fault; maybe he realised that I didn't really love him. Although I tried, I really tried.'

She fell silent, her eyes haunted as she remembered. Sam swore under his breath and put a hand on her arm. 'That's over, Francesca. We can start fresh.'

'No!' She shook him off with a violent gesture. 'Can't you see that it would never work? I'm afraid to let myself love anybody. I've been hurt twice and I just couldn't take it if it happened again.'

'But you can trust me, my darling,' Sam said urgently.

She shook her head. 'No. I'm never going to get married again.'

His tone cutting, Sam said, 'Well, thanks for the vote of confidence. Don't you have any courage, Francesca? Are you going to live like a coward all your life?'

Her mouth firmed. 'A woman doesn't have to have a man to lead a full and happy life. Not any more.'

Sam stared at her, then said shortly, 'So just why did you take me out to the vineyard last night?'

She bit her lip, knowing that she was going to make him angry. 'I thought that if we could just make love, then maybe you'd see it the way I did. I thought that you wouldn't be able to see things straight until—until we'd got the sex part of it out of the way.'

'So you intended it to happen?'

'Yes.'

A bitter look came into Sam's eyes. 'Was that all last night meant to you—just sex?' He gave a harsh laugh. 'Maybe you're right, Francesca. You're sure as hell mixed up if you can't tell the difference between that and love.' He slid off the bed and stood up. 'Are there any clothes here I could borrow?'

She looked away from his strongly masculine and yet vulnerable nakedness. 'Lennox stays here sometimes. He keeps some spare clothes in the other bedroom. They should fit...' Her words faded as she realised that Sam had already walked out of the door.

He came back fully dressed, wearing one of Lennox's suits. Picking up his keys and discarded clothes, he paused to look down at her, then merely said, 'So long, Francesca. It was—an experience knowing you.'

'I'll see you at dinner tonight.'

But he only shook his head with a grim smile, then walked out of the door.

When he'd gone Francesca leaned back in the bed for a time and convinced herself that he didn't mean it. He

couldn't, after last night. It had been so fantastic—better
than anything she had thought possible. No, he would
maybe be angry for a few hours but he would be back,
unable to keep away. No man could when he had the
opportunity for a similar night of passion, Francesca
thought rather cynically. No, Sam would be in her bed
again tonight, and every night that he was in Madeira.
And during those long hours of lovemaking she would
persuade him to accept the relationship she was offering, to take and demand nothing more than she was
prepared to give.

Feeling more confident, Francesca bathed, dressed and
had a leisurely brunch before driving over to the house.
Elaine was still there, out in the grounds overseeing the
dismantling of the marquee, checking invoices from the
various tradesmen they had used, doing the hundred and
one things that seemed to be part of her job, but always
organised, always cool.

'Are you going to stay on in Madeira for a few days?'
Francesca asked her.

'I can't, unfortunately; I have to get back to organise
a couple of weddings and a coming-of-age party next
week.'

'You sound really busy.'

'I am. The business is going far better than I expected—thanks a great deal to you and the contacts
you've given me,' Elaine said with a smile. 'Why don't
you come back to England with me and help, if you've
got nothing better to do?'

'I'd like that, but I've promised Calum that I'll go to
New York and organise some sort of bicentenary party
there. It will only be something quite small—nothing like
the celebrations here and in Portugal.'

They chatted for a while longer, then Francesca went into the house, her nerves tingling at the thought of seeing Sam again. She would have to play it very carefully, of course, but she was confident that she would soon be able to persuade him out of his angry mood, enough to make him agree to come to her tonight at least. But when she saw Stella and asked her where Sam was the other girl gave her an odd look.

'Why, Francesca, I thought you knew. Sam's gone. I thought you must have quarrelled or something,' she added, seeing Francesca's suddenly stricken face. 'He just packed his things and caught the first plane out.'

CHAPTER EIGHT

FRANCESCA didn't stay in Madeira. She went to her flat in Rome for a few days then flew to New York, where she was to organise the party and act as hostess. It turned out to be a double celebration because while she was in America word came that Stella had given birth to a boy. Lennox phoned the news through himself, his voice exultant with happiness.

Lennox naturally wanted some time to be with Stella and the baby, so Calum took over from him in Madeira for a while instead of coming to the party in New York. Originally Francesca had been looking forward to being in sole charge of organising this, but she found that the fun had somehow gone out of it. To strangers and casual acquaintances she still appeared vital and charming, but Chris noticed almost at once that something was wrong.

'Is it Sam?' he came right out and asked.

She shrugged and said obliquely, 'I can't think why you invited him to Madeira. You made him think I might be interested in him when I wasn't.' Abruptly she changed the subject. 'I hope you're not thinking of bringing Tiffany to the company party, Chris, because if you are I'll walk out.'

He gave her an exasperated look. 'Don't you have any tolerance? You liked Tiffany when you first met her; you could still if you weren't both so damn stubborn.'

'*Both* of us?'

'She's as set against you as you are against her.'

'Which is probably the only thing we'll ever agree on. Do you promise not to bring her?'

Chris was about to argue further, but he saw again the strained look about her eyes and decided not to goad her. 'All right, if you insist.'

The party went smoothly enough, was considered a success, and was written up in the society columns. Francesca had hoped that Tiffany would read the reports and be annoyed that she'd been kept away, but Chris said she was ill and couldn't have come anyway. Because of this Francesca saw little of him while she was in New York. She was staying with a girlfriend and spent a lot of time shopping and looking up friends, filling her time, trying to keep very busy.

A few days before she was due to leave she called Chris at his apartment but got Tiffany instead. It led to a row, of course. Tiffany was pert and wouldn't put Chris on the line, so Francesca accused her of taking Chris for everything she could get out of him. 'You're ruining his life,' she flung at Tiffany.

A few choice insults were exchanged, Tiffany saying tauntingly, 'What's the matter, Francesca, having man trouble—trouble in finding one that you can walk all over now that Michel has ditched you?'

'I have *not* been ditched,' Francesca returned furiously. 'It was the other way round. Michel was very sweet, but I——' Suddenly realising she was on the defensive, Francesca lost her temper, called Tiffany a disgusting little tramp, and slammed down the phone.

When she called again some time later it was Chris who answered. Francesca told him what she thought of Tiffany in very definite terms, but Chris interrupted quite brusquely, although he was willing enough to meet her for lunch before she left New York.

A few days later she went to the restaurant to meet him, but earlier than they'd first fixed as Chris had left a message asking her to bring the time forward. He hadn't arrived when she got there so she sat at a table to wait. But it was Tiffany who arrived a few minutes later, looking as chic and shiny as a new fashion doll.

Francesca's first thought was that Chris must be ill or something, so she said sharply, 'Has anything happened to Chris?'

'No, he's fine. I wanted to talk to you before he came.'

This meant that Tiffany had been responsible for altering the time. Francesca immediately tried to leave, but Tiffany said that she wanted to help her, that she'd learnt something of great importance to her, adding, 'I really think you ought to stay and listen.'

Reading menace in that, frightened for Chris and suspecting blackmail, Francesca sat back in her chair. 'Is this something to do with Chris?'

But Tiffany surprised her by saying, 'No, with you.' Then she surprised her even more when she said, 'Look, your marriage—did you go into it on the rebound?'

'*What*?' Francesca exclaimed in shocked anger.

'Were you in love with someone else, someone you—lost?'

Francesca stared at her, completely shaken, her first love brought shatteringly back to her mind. But Tiffany couldn't know about him, and mustn't be allowed to see that she was vulnerable. 'What the hell are you talking about? And just what right do you think you have to ask me such personal questions anyway?'

Again Tiffany said that she wanted to help her, but Francesca, really angry now, told her she didn't need help, especially not from Tiffany. Then she said venomously, 'How dare you presume on your—your dirty little liaison with Chris to meddle in my life?' She went on to berate the other girl for making the most of Chris's obsession with her, told her how it was playing havoc with Chris's working life, making him stay out of the office and cancel business trips, and that she, Francesca, had hardly seen him. Tiffany protested, but Francesca said, 'It was you who deliberately kept him away from me—out of spite.'

Her temper completely lost now, Francesca would have gone on to say a whole lot more, but Tiffany cut in, saying clearly, 'It's about Andrew Sims.'

Francesca looked quickly away, stunned by hearing the name of her first love, the student who'd walked out on her so long ago. So Tiffany did know! Her first panic-stricken thought was that Tiffany was trying to blackmail her and that she must give nothing away, not let the other girl see that she could be hurt. So she pretended not to recognise the name, saying 'Who?' as offhandedly as she could. Then she quickly turned defence into attack. 'Don't try and change the subject. Just get away from Chris. And get out of our lives!' she said furiously, hoping the anger would hide the vulnerability in her voice and manner.

Tiffany glared at her, a look of utter revulsion on her face, but to Francesca's deep relief she didn't mention Andy Sims again. Getting to her feet, Tiffany said vehemently, 'Nothing would give me more pleasure. You and your precious family are all the same— arrogant, conceited, heartless parasites! And for your information I can't *wait* to get away from Chris—because I hate him just as much as I hate the rest of the Brodeys!'

Tiffany's voice had risen, making people look round at them. Full of shocked indignation, Francesca only half took in what Tiffany was saying. The other girl turned away, and it was only then that they noticed Chris standing behind her. He said something very short, very curt. Tiffany looked at him mutinously for a moment, then shrugged and strode out of the restaurant, her head held high.

Francesca watched her go as Chris sat down in Tiffany's vacated chair. She turned to tell him what Tiffany had been saying, but something in his face, a grim sort of wretchedness, made anger fade to compassion. 'Did you—hear what she said?' she asked hesitatingly.

'Yes.'

She gave him a disturbed look. 'If she hates you so much, then—then there can only be one reason why she stays with you, Chris.'

'You don't have to tell me that,' he said shortly. He beckoned a waiter over. 'Let's order.'

They didn't talk much during the meal. Several times Francesca looked at Chris anxiously, worried for him, but knowing that she mustn't interfere.

When they'd almost finished, Chris said, 'Why did Tiffany come here? Did you ask her to? Were you trying to persuade her to leave me?'

'No! Someone left a message asking me to come earlier. It was supposed to be from you, but it must have been Tiffany. I don't know why. She said she wanted to help me but——' She broke off abruptly. Could it possibly have been true: had Tiffany really wanted to give her information about Andy? Did she know something about him? But why would she? Tiffany was far more likely to demand blackmail money than offer help. Wasn't she?

Francesca's mind and conscience stirred uneasily as she remembered the look of revulsion on Tiffany's face.

Was it possible that she'd got it all wrong? But then it occurred to her to wonder how on earth had Tiffany found out about Andy. Chris must have told her, she supposed. Indignant at having her secrets revealed, she almost asked Chris, but he was still sitting with that brooding look of unhappiness around his mouth and she didn't want to give him more worries.

When she left Chris, Francesca couldn't get Andy's name out of her mind. That evening, having dinner with the college friend with whom she was staying, she deliberately brought the conversation round to those days, the people they'd known. 'Did you ever hear what happened to Andy Sims?' she asked casually.

'No, he never turned up at any of the reunions. Although I think his address and telephone number are in my year book, if you want to call him.'

'Oh, good heavens, no.' Francesca changed the subject and again determined to put Andy out of her life as completely as he had put himself out of hers.

The reports of the celebration party had been out for quite some time now. If Sam had read them he would know she was in New York and might get in touch with her through the company office. She didn't particularly want him to phone her, of course, but she'd instructed the office to pass on her friend's number in case he did. She thought he might; that night they'd spent together had been so good that surely—— She bit her lip, cutting off her thoughts.

He didn't call.

A few days after meeting Chris, Francesca flew back to France to spend some time with her parents, and as soon as she arrived she phoned Calum, who was back in Oporto, and had a long talk to him about Chris, begging him to try to do something about Tiffany. 'She's making Chris so unhappy,' she told him. 'We can't just stand by and let it go on.'

'All right,' Calum said resignedly. 'I'll see what I can do.'

She didn't hear from him for a while, but then he rang one evening. 'I'm in New York,' he told her. 'I went to the apartment today and I saw Tiffany. I offered her money to leave Chris.'

He paused and Francesca guessed what he was going to say. 'She wouldn't take it.'

'No. I think she's trying to persuade Chris to marry her.'

'Oh, Calum, no!'

'I'm going to be in North America for a couple more weeks; perhaps I'll try again later.'

Francesca didn't have much hope that he'd succeed. She grew tired of France and went to Rome, but found the heat stifling so moved on to Oporto to stay with her grandfather.

It was there that Calum found her. She hadn't expected him and ran to greet him with a cry of pleasure when she saw him walking across the garden to where she was sitting by the pool.

He gave her a hug, but there was a strained look in his face. 'I have Chris with me.'

'Chris?' As she looked into his face her heart filled with fear. 'You don't mean that he's going to marry Tiffany? Is that why he's here?'

'No, the opposite. They've broken up.'

'Oh, but that's wonderful!' Francesca's face started to light up but when she saw Calum's expression she said, 'What is it?'

'Come inside, Francesca. We have to talk to you.'

Filled with apprehension, she tied a beach-wrap sarong-style round her waist and followed him into the sitting-room. Chris was standing by the window, waiting. There was a grim look to his face, a bleakness in his eyes, that tore at her heart. Going to him, she held him close for a moment, then he pulled her down beside him on to a sofa, and kept hold of her hand.

Standing opposite, Calum said, 'Francesca, it appears that before she left Tiffany took some documents from the safe in the apartment. Family papers. Chris has reason to believe that she sold those papers, along with an article she's written about us, to some gossip magazine. Unfortunately we don't yet know which one.'

'What papers?' she asked, mystified. 'And why on earth should any magazine be interested in them?'

Not answering directly, Calum said, 'One of the papers concerned you.'

Her head came up swiftly. 'Paolo?'

'No. Do you remember you once wanted to marry when you were in college? A boy called Andy Sims?'

She stared at him, remembering that Tiffany had known that name, and slowly nodded.

'You may remember Grandfather meeting him.' Calum cleared his throat, not liking what he had to say. 'Grandfather had only your best interests at heart. He instructed me to see if Sims was really serious about you or whether he could be bought off.' He paused, so that it was hardly necessary to say into the silence, 'He could. I paid him to leave college, stay out of your life.'

Chris's hand gripped hers. 'I'm sorry, Francesca. I didn't know the papers were missing until after she'd gone.'

'We're still trying to get them back, to stop the story from being printed. If we can just——'

'Why didn't you tell me?' Francesca cut in. 'You had no right to do what you did! And no right not to tell me afterwards.'

'We were trying to protect you.'

'Well, you didn't!' She stood up in a sudden rage and cried out, 'You destroyed me!'

Turning from them, she ran up to her room and locked herself in. Some time later Calum came up and knocked on the door but she wouldn't open it or come out. She sat in a chair, her knees drawn up in front of her, trying to come to terms with the way her life had been manipulated by the people she loved most. It took a while for the anger to fade enough for her to see that if Andy had been capable of being bought then her grandfather had been right about him. But it had been up to her to find that out, not him! And even if he had saved her from one unsuitable marriage, it had sent her headlong into an even worse one with Paolo.

And now it was all to come out into the open, the shameful little secret that people would pick over and laugh about. Tiffany must have known that time in the restaurant in New York. Had she wanted money? Would she have given up the papers if she'd been paid then? But Francesca remembered now that she had lost her temper and called Tiffany a lot of names. Was that why the other girl had written her slimy article? Was it not only to get money but for revenge as well?

Francesca shuddered, knowing well enough what it was like to be featured in magazines for the salacious. But Andy Sims would have his life affected by this too. And serve him damn well right, she thought vengefully, but then sighed, realising that Andy might be married and have a family, and it was hardly fair on them; he would have to be warned.

Getting to her feet, she showered and dressed, then packed a case.

It was easy enough to find Andy. All it took was a phone call to her college friend in New York, then a call to Andy's mother, who had given her the address in California. It seemed that Andy was working as a sports coach at a holiday inn on the coast. Francesca booked into a neighbouring complex, pushed her hair up under a baseball hat, donned a pair of dark glasses and, with unquiet mind, went to look up her old flame.

She found him on the tennis-court, giving lessons to a small group of women. He was still tall, good-looking, and she expected her heart to start to pound or at least to miss a beat, but it didn't. Sitting in a chair in a bar overlooking the practice court, a drink in her hand, Francesca watched him. He wasn't as lean as he had been when she'd known him; good living had made him fleshier. But the charmingly boyish, slightly crooked smile was still there and he used it often. And the women loved it, especially the more impressionable younger girls.

When the lesson ended they clustered round him to thank him before leaving. He called one woman back— not the prettiest or the youngest, but one wearing a lot of jewellery—and put his arms around her as he purported to show her what was wrong with her serve. Then they left the court together and came up to the bar for a drink.

Turning her back on them, Francesca pretended to be engrossed in the match on another court but listened avidly, and wasn't at all surprised to hear that the woman was alone. Andy, exuding all his charm, asked her for a date—an offer which was, of course, accepted.

Finishing her drink, Francesca walked away, finding herself strangely unmoved to learn that the man she had pined for, who had broken her heart and left it scarred, had turned out to be nothing but a cheap stud.

She didn't warn him about his impending notoriety; he looked the type who would probably enjoy it.

Back at her hotel, Francesca felt as if a great weight had lifted from her shoulders. She saw her life since Andy had walked out, the things she'd done, in an entirely new perspective now. And values; those too had changed dramatically. For some time she thought of her past, realising how and why she'd made the mistake of marrying Paolo. So what of the future? She didn't think about that for very long. Reaching for the phone, she called Calum.

'Francesca! Are you all right? We've been worried about you.'

'Yes, I'm fine. *Really* fine. Calum, do you have Sam's number?'

With laughter in his voice, he said, 'I've been carrying it around with me, just waiting for you to ask that question.'

Sam's voice sounded very close when he picked up the phone. Francesca's chest felt tight about her pounding heart and it was a moment before she could say huskily, 'Hello, Sam.'

There was a pause and she thought he hadn't recognised her voice, but then he said on a guarded note, 'Hello, Princess.'

'How—how are you?'

'What do you want, Princess?'

So he wasn't going to help her at all. Her voice unsteady, she said, 'You once invited me to stay. I—I'd like to take you up on your offer.'

Again there was silence, then Sam said, 'Get a plane to Cheyenne. Bring some riding clothes with you.' And he put down the phone.

When Francesca arrived in Cheyenne the next day she expected to find Sam waiting for her, having phoned and left a message giving her arrival time, but instead she was met by an entirely different man. Middle-aged, laconic, he picked up her bags and led her out to another plane, a small private jet this time. It turned out that he was the pilot and she the only passenger.

They flew on for another couple of hours, high above the clouds most of the time, but what scenery Francesca did see was so magnificent that it had her riveted to the window. High mountains and glaciers, plains that seemed to go on forever, huge forests; it was breathtaking in its wild beauty.

Francesca had never been to Wyoming before, knew little about it beyond the fact that it had several national parks, including the famous Yellowstone. She would have liked to ask the pilot if they were flying over it, but he had closed the door of the cockpit, firmly shutting her out after instructing her to fasten her safety belt.

Finally, the plane began to descend and Francesca looked out, expecting to see an airport below her, but they seemed to be in an area of sparse forest with, not far away, the foothills of some mountains. She wondered if she ought to start worrying, but then glimpsed the long stretch of a tarmac runway before the pilot straightened the plane and they came smoothly in to land. The pilot taxied towards the only building in sight—a wooden, barn-like structure—and switched off the engine. Alongside the barn was a small fenced paddock with horses in it. Francesca looked round with some be-

musement as she climbed down from the plane, but then
the door of the barn opened and Sam came out.

It was the man she knew, her lover, and yet completely unlike him. Gone were the smart casual clothes
that he'd worn in Portugal and Madeira; instead he wore
faded denim jeans, an open-necked shirt and denim
jacket. There were heeled riding-boots on his feet and a
far from new stetson pushed back on his head. He looked
her over but had no smile or word of greeting; he just
said, 'Did you bring some riding clothes?'

'Yes.' Francesca gestured towards the pilot who was
carrying her cases from the plane.

'You can change in the barn.' He handed her a pair
of saddle-bags. 'Put everything you need for a couple
of days in these—and don't bring more than you need.'
And then he went over to speak to the pilot.

Francesca gazed after him for a moment, not sure if
she liked being ordered about like this. But then she took
one of her cases into the barn and changed into jeans
and a casual shirt. It was easy enough to decide what to
wear now; deciding what to take with her was a whole
lot harder. The saddle-bags were bulging by the time
she'd stowed as much as possible into them and came
out of the barn.

The plane was just taking off, rising into the air and
circling round before disappearing into the sky. Beside
the paddock two horses were standing, already saddled.
Sam took the saddle-bags from her, grimaced at their
weight, and immediately opened them up and started
taking things out.

'You won't need this,' he said, pulling out a gorgeous
nightdress that she had bought only yesterday. 'Or this.'
Out came her make-up bag. 'And you certainly won't
need these.' And he tossed aside her shampoo and shower

stuff and a spare pair of shoes. 'You can pack that lot back in your case,' he ordered.

Francesca didn't move. She looked down at him where he crouched to do up the bags and said in sardonic self-mockery, 'Well, hello, Francesca, how delightful to see you again.'

Glancing up, Sam's mouth twisted into a wry smile. He finished fastening the saddle-bags, stood up and merely said, 'Let's get going.'

'Where?'

'You'll see.'

'What about my cases?'

'They'll be safe enough in the barn.'

Francesca looked at him for a moment, then took her things and put them back in her suitcase. She supposed she should have expected this, she thought resignedly. After all, the last time she had seen him she had thrown Sam's proposal back in his face, had as good as told him he wasn't the man for her, and now here she was, having turned up more or less out of the blue, expecting him to welcome her with open arms. It was hardly any wonder he was playing it cool.

Emerging from the barn, she found him waiting by one of the horses, a handsome palomino mare. 'Ever ridden with a western saddle before?'

'No. Is it difficult?'

'You'll soon get used to it. I'll give you a leg-up.'

She could probably have managed by herself, but Francesca let him help her because she wanted, needed him to touch her. But his hands didn't linger once she was safely in the saddle. He moved to unhitch his own horse—a big bay—got into the saddle with one easy, fluid movement, and began to lead her away from the air-strip. Francesca had to concentrate on this new way of riding, but once she got used to not rising in the saddle she found it surprisingly comfortable.

They were slowly climbing, weaving through pine trees or crossing open land, but it was a while before she was confident enough to take in the scenery. The horizon seemed far away, the tree-covered slopes of the foothills rising to the dark grey of mountains topped by ridges of white where the sun shone on the snow. At their feet there were wild flowers, millions of them, yellow and purple and red: the hills were ablaze with colour.

And it was so quiet; only the sound of the horses, their hooves gently thudding on the grass, the rhythmic rasp of their breath, the occasional metallic jingle of the bridles, seemed to break the silence. It took a while for Francesca's city ears to hear the other sounds: the tinkling flow of a stream, the call of a bird, the soft rustle in the undergrowth where some small animal hurried from their path.

Sam had been riding ahead of her but she spurred her horse alongside him now. 'Have you always lived here, Sam?' she asked him.

He nodded and gestured towards the west. 'I was born about twenty miles from here—same place as my father and grandfather.'

'In the ranch-house?'

He glanced at her, looking for mockery, perhaps, but she was regarding him steadily. 'That's right.'

'Do your parents still live there?'

'No. They're both dead.'

'I'm sorry,' she said in quick, genuine sympathy.

Sam shrugged. 'It was a while ago.'

'Tell me about your ranch, Sam.'

But he only smiled a little and said, 'Some time, maybe.' They were approaching trees again and he pulled ahead.

They rode on for another hour, not talking much, stopping once to watch a herd of white-tailed deer that had gathered at a stream to drink, the sun dappling the rich chestnut of their backs. When a snort by one of the horses frightened them they went careering off through the trees, and Francesca laughed delightedly, turning a glowing face to Sam. For the first time he smiled back at her, but then turned abruptly away as if regretting even that small lapse.

Francesca was beginning to feel tired as muscles that weren't used to this style of riding started to ache, when they rounded a fold in the hills and she saw a log cabin built on a small plateau of flat land, sheltered from the winds by the surrounding hills. They stopped outside and she climbed stiffly down.

There was just one room to the cabin. It had a stove, table and chairs, and one bed, not very wide, already made up with blankets. Intriguing.

Sam didn't use the stove; he built a fire outside, hung a billy-can for coffee over it, and cooked a meal of steak and beans on the flames.

It was only when they had eaten that he began to talk, and then it was not about himself but about Wyoming. He told her how rough the winters could be, with below-zero temperatures, deep snows, and deadly blizzards that could blow any time between November and June. He told her of great winds in the plains, often of sixty miles an hour or more, and then there were always the summer rainstorms.

'It's a place of extremes,' he told her. 'Intense heat, freezing cold. There are floods, dust storms, forest fires; you name it, to us it's commonplace.'

She was aware that he was trying to put her off, testing her, perhaps. 'Why stay here, then?' she asked lightly.

'It's home, I guess.'

'It couldn't be because the mountains are so grand and awesome, because the air is clean and invigorating, because there are so few people, could it?'

He gave a short laugh. 'That too.' He got to his feet, went over to make sure the horses were OK, and came back with a bed-roll from his saddle. 'I'll sleep out here,' he told her. 'You can take the cabin.'

She didn't move, just looked up at him and said, 'Are you punishing me, Sam?' He didn't answer and she put up a hand to her hair. 'I suppose I deserve it if you are. But don't you want to know why I came here, why I wanted to see you?'

Going to the fire, he threw on another log. Not looking at her, he said, 'Why, then?'

'It's a long story—and not a very nice one. Will you listen?'

He sat down on the opposite side of the fire. 'Sure, I'll listen,' he answered, but his voice wasn't encouraging.

So she told him about Andy Sims and the way he'd been bought off, the effect it had had on her life. And, glad of the darkness so that he couldn't see her face, she told him about Paolo. Not all of it, because some of it was too painful to tell, but enough for him to realise what a hell it had been. 'So you see,' she said, 'I didn't trust love, or even myself. I thought it must be something in me. I was afraid to risk myself, my feelings, ever again.'

'And now?'

'Now I know the truth—well, I'm still afraid. But I'm willing to try.'

Sam was silent for a moment, then said heavily, 'You can't change overnight, Francesca. So you found out the truth about your old boyfriend; maybe you're on the rebound from that. A few weeks here and you'll be bored out of your mind. You won't be able to kick the dust of Wyoming off your boots and hightail it back to Europe fast enough.'

'Maybe that's true,' she admitted. 'I don't know. Maybe we'll both have to compromise.' Her voice faltered, then gathered strength. 'But one thing I do know: I've missed you most dreadfully, Sam. I think about you—and long for you all the time. I tried hard not to; I admit that. But my life is so empty without you. I looked into the future and there seemed no point in living it, not alone, not without you.'

She paused, wanting him to speak, but when he didn't she went on, 'You asked me to come here, to see what your life was like. I don't think it really matters any more what your life is like here; I only know that *I* don't have a life, not unless I'm with you.' She looked at him across the embers of the dying fire and said softly, bravely, 'I love you, Sam.'

He stood up and poured a can of water over the fire, making it hiss and spit into darkness. 'Go to bed, Francesca,' he said shortly.

'Will you come with me?'

His answer was curt. 'No.'

'Why not?'

'It's too soon. You aren't—sure enough of yourself yet.'

'I know I want you.'

'That has nothing to do with it.'

Seeing that he was implacable, she got to her feet and went into the cabin. Sam came with her to light the lamp.

'Don't you have a patchwork quilt for the bed? All log cabins should have at least one.' She swung round as he went to leave. 'Kiss me goodnight, Sam.'

In the light of the lamp she could see that his face, his body were very tense. He had taken off his hat and was more the man she remembered now, the man who had taken her so gloriously that night among the vines. He took a half-step towards her, then hesitated, shook his head. It came to her that having her so close must be as hard for him as it was for her, perhaps more so. She had rebuffed him twice; he would have to be very sure of her before he would allow himself to relax his iron self-control. She could understand how he felt, realised how it would hurt him if she changed her mind, if she didn't love him enough and left him.

But Francesca knew she wouldn't do that and had tried to tell him so. Her nature might not change—there might be times when she had to get away for a while to the life she had been brought up to—but she knew with the utmost certainty that she would never leave Sam, never stop loving him. It might be a crazy mixture of a marriage, but she'd make darn sure it was a good one.

She tried to put her feelings into her eyes, but Sam turned away. 'Better get some sleep,' he said tersely. 'We'll be making an early start in the morning.'

He went out and shut the door. Francesca undressed slowly, taking off all her clothes, brushing out her hair and washing herself from the bowl of water Sam had poured for her earlier. She dried herself on the rough but clean towel, her thoughts on Sam, so close physically but so far away in his obstinacy. There was a noise outside the cabin, a sort of scraping sound, and stories of grizzly bears sprang to her mind before she realised it was a branch scraping the roof in the breeze. The noise didn't come again and she slowly relaxed, but then an idea came to her.

Pulling the blanket from the bed, she wrapped it round herself, waited for a while, until she thought Sam would be asleep in his bed-roll, then let out a terrific scream, the noise rending the silence of the night.

Sam couldn't have been asleep, he was in there so fast. 'What is it?' he yelled.

'I think I'm dying.'

'Francesca!' He sprang towards her, fear and consternation in his face.

She let the blanket drop and stood there naked before him, the lamplight playing on the curves of her body, on the length of her legs. Her long blonde hair fell to curl across her breasts, tantalisingly, half hiding her nipples. Sam gave a great gasp and stopped precipitately in front of her.

'Dying from frustration,' she said softly. 'From wanting you.' She moved forward, put her hands on his chest. 'Don't let me die, Sam. Please don't let me die.' Her hands moved upwards, caressed the back of his neck, weaved their way into his hair. Her legs moved against his, her lips reached up to caress his mouth, the tip of her tongue flicking out to explore its softness.

Sam caught her wrists, went to pull her arms down, but she gently bit his lip, then kissed him with fierce passion. He groaned deep in his throat, his hands tightened, but the next moment his arms went round her and he was returning her kiss, returning it a hundredfold.

He tore himself away from her and held her at arm's length. Francesca gave a cry almost of despair. 'Oh, Sam, no! Please don't go. Stay with me.'

His voice thick and rough, he said, 'No... I just want to look at you.' His eyes went over her, lingering, glorying in her beauty. 'Oh, Francesca. You're so incredibly lovely.' He gave a deep sigh. 'You witch. You temptress. You know darn well I can't resist you.' His gaze lifted to her face. 'It's been hell, waiting for you to call, scared to death that you wouldn't, telling myself what a fool I was not to stay with you in Madeira. How I could have been with you, making love to you. Leaving you there was the hardest thing I've ever done in my life, but I *had* to do it. I needed your total commitment, Francesca.' He paused. 'I still need it.'

'You have it,' she said softly. 'My love, my heart, my life—they're all yours. If you'll have me.'

He gave a soft laugh. 'You stand there like a rose in the desert, so beautiful, so much a woman—and you ask me *if* I'll have you!' He drew her to him, looked deep into her eyes. 'For the third and last time, Francesca, will you marry me?'

She smiled and put up a hand to caress his cheek. 'Yes, and yes, and yes, my dearest love, my love for now and always.'

He kissed her compulsively, then put his hands up to undo his shirt, but she stopped him. 'No, let me do it for you,' she said eagerly.

He groaned as her fingers slid the shirt from his shoulders and wandered across his chest, gasped as she undid his belt and zip and slipped her hands inside his jeans to guide them down his legs. His breath became a hoarse, panting moan as she touched him, kissed him, until, with a cry, Sam pulled her to him, his need desperate, their naked bodies swaying in the lamplight as they kissed with joyous passion. Swinging her up into his arms, he carried her to the bed, where they came together at last with all the abandonment of complete trust and love.

Francesca glanced down for one last look at the ranch as the same small jet-plane that had brought her here flew over the house. It had become so familiar in the last few weeks, become her home. But now they were on the first leg of their journey back to Oporto where they were to be married in a civil ceremony with all her family present. Then they would stay with Grandfather for a couple of weeks before returning to Wyoming for another wedding ceremony and celebration, for all Sam's people this time.

No magazine article about her had appeared yet, not that Francesca cared any more, unless it bothered Sam. His happiness was her first consideration now.

She was alone in the passenger cabin again; Sam, unable to resist, was flying the plane—his plane. And when she looked out of the window, almost all the territory she could see belonged to him. It had come as quite a revelation to learn of the empire his family had built—in oil, tourism, ranching, business—which he controlled. One which, she was pretty certain, made the Brodey empire look quite small by comparison. When Sam had said that he could take care of her, he had really meant it.

His basic character was true and straight, as she had always known it, but she was learning new, fascinating things about him all the time. As he was about her, she supposed. Because she had changed while she'd been here with Sam. The restlessness that had driven her to marry Paolo, to excesses of partying and shopping, had gone, along with her inhibitions and doubts about herself. Her confidence now was real, not an act to deceive herself and the world. And she had never been so happy, so content. Happiness shone out of her like a radiant light. She was a tigress tamed, sleek and beautiful in the sun.

The plane landed at Cheyenne and they walked through to the airport to check in their bags for the flight to New York where they were to spend the night. They sat together in the departure lounge, waiting for their flight to be called; sat close, her hand in his. 'We'll have tonight and all tomorrow morning in New York,' Sam remarked. 'Would you like to take in a show tonight?'

Francesca gave him a provocative look. 'We've never made love in New York yet.'

Sam grinned delightedly. 'So we haven't. OK, that's tonight taken care of. But how about tomorrow morning? I expect you'd like to shop?'

Her eyebrows rose. 'When we could still be in bed? Besides——' she gave an eloquent shrug '—shopping? Who needs it?'

Sam gave a shout of laughter, making every head turn. Ignoring them all, he gave her an exuberant hug. 'Now I *know* you really love me!'

HARLEQUIN PRESENTS®

So who were the Brodeys?

Money, looks, style. The Brodey family
had everything...except love

in

Sally Wentworth's exciting three-part series
TIES OF PASSION

Read Calum Brodey's story in

#1843 CALUM

Harlequin Presents—the best has just
gotten better!

Available in October wherever Harlequin books
are sold.

Look us up on-line at: http://www.romance.net

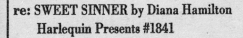

HARLEQUIN PRESENTS®

PENNY JORDAN

"Penny Jordan pens a formidable read."
—*Romantic Times*

Harlequin brings you the best books by the best authors!

Watch for:
#1839 THE TRUSTING GAME

Christa had learned the hard way that men were not to be trusted. So why should she believe Daniel when he said he could teach her to trust?

Harlequin Presents—the best has just gotten better!
Available in October wherever
Harlequin books are sold.

Look us up on-line at: http://www.romance.net

TAUTH-13

HARLEQUIN®

Don't miss these Harlequin favorites by some of our most
distinguished authors!
And now, you can receive a discount by ordering two or more titles!

HT #25663	THE LAWMAN by Vicki Lewis Thompson	$3.25 U.S. ☐/$3.75 CAN. ☐
HP #11788	THE SISTER SWAP by Susan Napier	$3.25 U.S. ☐/$3.75 CAN. ☐
HR #03293	THE MAN WHO CAME FOR CHRISTMAS by Bethany Campbell	$2.99 U.S. ☐/$3.50 CAN. ☐
HS #70667	FATHERS & OTHER STRANGERS by Evelyn Crowe	$3.75 U.S. ☐/$4.25 CAN. ☐
HI #22198	MURDER BY THE BOOK by Margaret St. George	$2.89 ☐
HAR #16520	THE ADVENTURESS by M.J. Rodgers	$3.50 U.S. ☐/$3.99 CAN. ☐
HH #28885	DESERT ROGUE by Erin Yorke	$4.50 U.S. ☐/$4.99 CAN. ☐

(limited quantities available on certain titles)

	AMOUNT	$
DEDUCT:	**10% DISCOUNT FOR 2+ BOOKS**	$
ADD:	**POSTAGE & HANDLING**	$
	($1.00 for one book, 50¢ for each additional)	
	APPLICABLE TAXES**	$_____
	TOTAL PAYABLE	$_____
	(check or money order—please do not send cash)	

To order, complete this form and send it, along with a check or money order for the
total above, payable to Harlequin Books, to: **In the U.S.:** 3010 Walden Avenue,
P.O. Box 9047, Buffalo, NY. 14269-9047; **In Canada:** P.O. Box 613, Fort Erie, Ontario,
L2A 5X3.

Name:_____

Address:_____ City:_____

State/Prov.:_____ Zip/Postal Code:_____

**New York residents remit applicable sales taxes.
  Canadian residents remit applicable GST and provincial taxes.   HBACK-JS3

Look us up on-line at: http://www.romance.net